The Type-A Guide to Solving Murder

A Sunset Ridge Cozy Mystery, Volume 1

Elizabeth Spann Craig

Published by Elizabeth Spann Craig, 2024.

THE TYPE-A GUIDE TO SOLVING MURDER

First edition. April 23, 2024.

Written by Elizabeth Spann Craig.

Chapter One

1. *Purchase drawer organizers*
2. *Research and retain a reliable yard service (ask neighbors?)*
3. *Visit the library and obtain a library card*
4. *Explore nearby parks*
5. *Figure out garbage collection days (ask neighbors?)*
6. *Purchase a welcome mat for the front door*
7. *Join a fitness class*
8. *Schedule a meet-and-greet with homeowner association president*
9. *Attend the Maple Hills picnic*

Samantha looked down at her list, tapping the paper with her favorite pen.

Her husband, Chad, looked wryly at her. "I know it's probably pointless to ask, but why don't you take a few minutes of downtime, Sam? You've been working like crazy the last three days." He gestured around their house, where the movers had just delivered the boxes and furniture several days earlier. "You've unpacked an entire house, and set everything up."

Samantha gave him a generous grin. "Hey, you've been helpful, yourself."

Chad snorted. "You gave me a box cutter and pointed out several boxes of plates and crystal. All I did was unpack them and put them into the cabinets you wanted them in."

Sam knew the fact of the matter was that she'd wanted to unpack everything herself. Chad was excellent at many things. But organizing their belongings in a new house would never be his strong suit. "I tell you what you can help me with. Actually, it would be a huge help."

Chad looked at her doubtfully. He absently pushed back the lock of brown hair that had fallen into his eyes. Sam thought that, considering him as objectively as she could, he was practically as youthful-looking as he'd been when she'd met him in college, although he was in his thirties. He looked as if he could be a returning fraternity brother at an alumni night. Preppy as usual, he wore a crisp, button-down Oxford shirt, khaki chinos, and classic loafers. Dressed as he was, the busywork she assigned him shouldn't get his hands dirty. That ruled out half the things she needed to get done.

Then she got it. "It would be a huge help if you ran to the store for me."

Chad brightened at this prospect. Perhaps he also imagined unpleasant and potentially messy scenarios. "The store? Sure. But didn't you go there yesterday?"

"Oh, I'm at the store nearly every day at this stage. But yesterday, I went out for shelf paper. Now I need food for the picnic this afternoon."

Chad's face fell comically. "The picnic? The Maple Hills one?" Maple Hills was a pleasant subdivision in the North Carolina mountain town of Sunset Ridge. Sunset Ridge was perched on top of a series of rolling hills and offered beautiful panoramic views of the surrounding peaks. It had a real mix of homes and residents. A few of the homes were mountain estates, similar to Sam and Chad's house. Others were small log cabins and large lodges. The town was a year-round residence for many, but others in warmer states came to escape the summer heat.

Sam nodded, adding a few quick items to the picnic-related list.

Chad said, "I'd totally forgotten about that. I guess we need to make an appearance."

It was spoken as more of a question. Sam said, "I think we definitely should. Everyone will be curious, of course. It's the perfect way to meet the rest of our neighbors. It's going to be a great way to connect."

"I'll never remember anyone's name," said Chad ruefully. "You remember what happened in Charlotte at that neighborhood party?"

Sam did. She'd thought it was very unsporting for their Charlotte neighbor to pretend to be someone completely different just because Chad had mistaken them for someone else.

"I'll make a cheat sheet after the picnic is over, with notes on appearances and names so you can memorize them."

Chad said dryly, "And quiz me over breakfast."

"Naturally." Sam tapped her pencil against her list again. "We're bringing deviled eggs and deli sandwiches. I'll order them from the store to make it easier. Then you only have to pick them up."

"Got it." He stretched, glancing around at the house. "This place was an empty shell a couple of days ago. You've really worked some magic in here."

Samantha shrugged. "That's because I'm not a perfectionist. Being a perfectionist slows people down."

Chad tilted his head to one side, his hair flopping into his face again. "You seem like a perfectionist to me. You jumped right in and unpacked for eight hours a day."

"No, that's really not being a perfectionist. That's just being Type-A. I wanted to get it done because I hate seeing boxes everywhere. A perfectionist would have probably moved items several times to find them the ideal spot. And a perfectionist would never have hung all the pictures on the walls in a single afternoon."

"I see," said Chad thoughtfully. He glanced around their sunroom, which stretched the entire length of the back of the house. The walls were dotted with various oil paintings and prints. "I did notice one of the pictures might be slightly off-kilter compared to the others."

Sam shrugged. "But it's on the wall. I didn't use a leveler or a measuring tape. I eyeballed them and put them up." She opened her laptop, single-minded again, and pulled up the grocery store's website. There, she ordered five sub sandwiches of various types and a container of deviled eggs. "They say the order will be ready in an hour."

Chad gave her a jaunty salute, grinning. "Got it."

Sam said, "Thanks. That's a big help."

Chad watched his wife as she ran a hand absently through her dark-brown hair. "I have the feeling you should put your feet up for a while, but I know better. You're crackling with energy."

"I'll try to read for a little while after I finish making these lists."

"What's our agenda for the picnic?" asked Chad.

Sam glanced up, looking innocent. "Agenda? What do you mean?"

"You usually have a plan for even the most innocent of gatherings. What's your ulterior motive for the neighborhood picnic?"

Sam quirked a brow at him. "You're making me sound like some sort of criminal mastermind."

"Nope. Just somebody who thinks ahead."

"Well, my thoughts right now are centered on the subs and deviled eggs. Very innocent things. But I do want us to meet as many people as we can and sort of get the scoop on the neighborhood. Find out who are the power players, for instance."

A smile tugged at Chad's lips. "Power players in the Maple Hills subdivision?"

"Sure, there are. I'm sure Maple Hills is like any other innocuous-seeming place. It's basically a microcosm of a city. You'll have the nosy neighbor, the HOA president desperate to cling to power, the super-nice neighbors who would give you the shirts off their backs. I'd like to know who all those people are, and more."

"I'm sensing there might be a political run in your future," said Chad with a smile.

A few hours went by, with Chad going to the store and Sam making lists and regularly knocking items off of them. She arranged the sandwiches Chad bought on a pretty plate, stacking them for height and visual interest. Then Sam wrote the type of sandwich on tiny toothpick flags and stuck them into the bread.

"Do I look all right?" asked Chad shortly before it was time to leave.

"You'll do," said Sam with a teasing look.

"And you look amazing, as always." Chad's voice was earnest.

Sam snorted. "Well, *I'll* do. We don't want to go over-the-top for a neighborhood picnic." It was warm outside, especially for September. She was wearing a knit, dark olive midi-length wrap dress, which set off her dark hair and complemented her slender form. But Sam's mind ran more to the practical—she hadn't wanted to sweat while meeting her new neighbors. And since they were walking to the picnic, keeping comfortable was key.

Chad carefully carried the tote bag of food as they strolled down the street toward the large pond at the center of the subdivision. As they approached, they saw thirty or more people gathered on the shores of the pond, under the firs providing relief from the sun.

"Where do we start?" asked Chad, looking uncharacteristically overwhelmed by the number of new neighbors milling around.

"I'm going to make a quick lap around," said Sam. "Could you set out the food on that picnic table?"

Chad did and was immediately absorbed into a small group of men who launched into a conversation involving home renovations, tools, and work.

Having done some research prior to the picnic, Sam knew who the homeowner association president was and had even found a picture of him online. George Turner was exactly the person she wanted to speak with. He was standing by himself, frowning as his gaze flicked around the gathering. She moved with some determination in his direction, wanting to ask about neighborhood activities and the general mood of Maple Hills. But George, seeing her coming, swiftly pivoted and engaged himself with a group of men. Sam blinked. Maybe he was shy about meeting new people?

Sam decided to drop back and punt. She glanced around the gathering, then strode up to an older woman with a dissatisfied expression on her face. Often, these types of women were the ones who knew everything that went on in a place. They were up on local gossip. And they offered completely unsolicited opinions on everything.

Sam extended her hand to the woman, smiling brightly. "Hi. I'm Samantha Prescott, but lots of people call me Sam. My husband and I just moved into the neighborhood."

The woman gave the proffered hand a sideways glance. "Sorry, I don't shake hands. Too many oddball germs and infections out there."

Sam quickly withdrew her hand, unable to stop herself from reflexively wiping her hand on her dress.

The woman primly stated, "I'm Nora Snodwick. I saw the moving vans, so I know you're living in the Terrys' old house. I live right down the street from you in number 52."

Sam could tell by the woman's tone that their moving vans had somehow represented some sort of burden. She gave her the bright smile again. "Were the vans loud?"

Nora appeared to be delighted to launch into the various failings of the moving company. "One of the men whistled tunes while he unloaded the truck. He had quite a *piercing* whistle. Then there was the music that they played during their lunch break. Very, very loud and quite objectionable music."

"I'm very sorry to hear that," said Sam.

"You didn't notice it yourself?" asked Nora, her tone faintly disbelieving.

Sam had been a lot more focused on ensuring the boxes made it into the correct rooms, finding the *vital* boxes that contained items she and Chad would need later in the day, and then taking her box cutter and releasing the vital items from their cardboard coverings. "I heard music, but I'll admit it sounded cheerful to me." Ready to change the subject from her moving company, Sam said in an admiring way, "You seem like someone who might really have your finger on the pulse of the neighborhood."

This made Nora puff up a bit with pride. "I suppose I do, yes. Let's just say that I'm observant."

"I'm guessing you're the star member of the neighborhood watch program."

Nora made a face, although her face had already been so bitter looking that it was hard to tell the difference.

"There's no neighborhood watch program here," she said with a sniff. "I've lobbied for it, but you know how it is here in Maple Hills."

Sam waited politely for the realization to hit Nora that Sam likely *didn't* know how things were in Maple Hills, having just moved in. When that realization didn't sink in, she said, "No, I really don't. I'd love some insights into the subdivision from a real insider."

Being called an insider clearly pleased Nora. She straightened up a bit. "Well, George Turner is the homeowner association president." She leaned in closer to Sam. "I *strongly* suspect that there's something illegal going on with the votes. Everyone I talk to swears they won't vote for George to lead the HOA and yet he somehow always stays in power." Nora's venomous gaze settled on George, who was currently speaking with Chad, the rest of the group of men having wandered off to other conversations. At any rate, Sam supposed Nora was glowering at George and not at Sam's husband.

"That's George?" asked Sam, nodding toward an attractive man in his late-fifties with rather cold eyes and a confident air. Naturally, she knew exactly who he was, but it was nice to both have confirmation and make Nora feel as if she were helpfully filling her in.

"That's him," said Nora, her voice dripping with animosity. "No one likes him."

Just to be a contrarian, Chad tipped his head back, laughing with enthusiasm at some witticism George made. Nora's eyes narrowed at Chad, as if suddenly suspecting he was very dim-witted.

Sam said, "It sounds like the HOA needs some fresh blood, then. At least in terms of the president." And, perhaps, someone a bit friendlier. It now sounded as if George hadn't been shy when he avoided her. It was decidedly more of a brush-off.

"Yes," said Nora sourly. "I've run for HOA president several times with no success. I'm positive the votes are being manipulated. The problem with George is that as soon as he knows you want any sort of architectural review on your house, he'll shut it down. Good luck if you want to build a fence or a deck on your property."

It sounded as if Nora could go on all day about George's iniquities. Sam, however, wanted more of an overview. She had the feeling Nora would be delighted to give her an in-depth opinion of the HOA any time Sam dropped by her house for a visit.

"How about the rest of the neighbors?" Sam asked lightly. It was why she chose Nora, with her dissatisfied expression, as the person she spoke with first. Most people, knowing she was new to the neighborhood, would have given her a very wholesome version of Maple Hills. That was decidedly what Sam didn't want.

Nora sniffed again. "A bunch of oddballs."

Sam glanced around the assembly. None of her new neighbors seemed to fit that designation. She saw a couple of smiling couples with young children running around their feet. There were neighbors, old and young. A few had brought their fur babies with them. Although Sam did notice a woman in her thirties with jet-black hair and a somewhat fragile appearance hanging back. She stood on the fringe of the picnic, near the pond, with an anxious expression on her face.

"That's one of the oddballs there," said Nora uncharitably. "Goes by Pris. Surely that's not the woman's real name. Must be a nickname. No one's mother saddles them with the name of Pris! But that's neither here nor there."

"Is Pris new to the neighborhood, too?" Sam figured that not everyone would jump into a crowd of unfamiliar faces as enthusiastically as she and Chad had done.

"You'd think so, wouldn't you? But she's been here for at least a year, maybe two. Pris rarely comes to these things, probably because she won't open her mouth the whole time she's here."

To Sam's alarm, Nora started pointing her finger, indicating various neighbors. "The Smiths don't roll their garbage containers from the street for days. The Browns are horrible pet owners who never bring their dog into the house. The Callahans keep their grass too long and have weeds growing out of their driveway." Nora continued reciting the various flaws of most of the people at the picnic.

But Sam was barely listening now. She was far more interested in the pale woman with auburn hair and athletic build who was having a furtive conversation with the problematic HOA president, George Turner, while Chad stood by, looking for other people to speak with. Then George said something to her, and she shrank away from him quickly.

Sam quickly gave Nora a warm smile. "You've been so helpful. I'd better grab something to eat and catch up with Chad."

Nora nodded, already drawing back and surveying the picnic as if deciding which victim to single out for her next conversation. She finally settled on a group of older women who looked decidedly displeased at her arrival.

The tables of food weren't far from the woman and George's conversation. Sam filled a plate with food while monitoring the two of them. George reached out a hand, and she shrank back from it. George walked away, looking satisfied. The woman's eyes filled with tears. A tall man now speaking with Chad was staring grimly at the woman.

Samantha joined a group of young mothers, to see what their impressions of Maple Hills were and how they differed from Nora's. She suspected the opinions would vary quite a bit and would involve glossing over any issues. A few minutes later, though, she found the mothers appeared more interested in Sam and Chad and the large house they'd moved into than divulging anything interesting about themselves or the subdivision.

Sam was about to excuse herself politely and find another group when she heard a call for help. Turning around, she saw George Turner, the HOA president, on the ground.

Chapter Two

She sprinted over there. "Someone call 911," she barked as everyone stared in horror at George's unconscious figure. Chad quickly took out his phone to make the call.

"Is there a healthcare worker here?" she called out loudly. Everyone silently shook their heads, but many stared at a young man who was frozen in place.

George's breath was uneven and wheezing. Sam checked to make sure he wasn't choking and adjusted his position to keep his airway was as clear as possible. It didn't seem to do any good. She spotted a bracelet on his wrist and turned it so that she could read it. The bracelet stated he was allergic to almonds. As George started turning blue, and his breathing became more labored, she said, "Can somebody help me look for an EpiPen? He might be having an allergic reaction."

Chad was still on the phone with the dispatcher. One of the young moms joined Sam in patting down George's pockets, looking for the EpiPen.

"You think he's in anaphylactic shock?" asked another of the women Sam had spoken with.

"He could be," said Sam, giving up her search for an EpiPen.

"This is his plate," she said, pointing to a paper plate next to George that had somehow fallen face-up. It appeared to be covered with a grainy salad.

Nora's gruff voice came from behind Sam. "He was allergic to almonds."

"Move the plate away from him," said Sam sharply. Then, to George, she said in a calm, reassuring voice, "You're okay. Help is on the way. Just hang on." She wasn't at all sure George could hear her.

"Is anyone certified in CPR?" Sam called out.

Another of the young mothers came over. "I just took the course."

"Then you'll be better than I am. It's been years," said Sam. She reached for George's pulse, which felt faint. "He's still breathing, but it's getting harder and harder for him." In the distance, she could hear a siren approaching.

The young mom started CPR as the ambulance pulled to the side of the road near the picnic. The EMTs took over once they arrived, loading George quickly into an ambulance. A younger man from the picnic crowd climbed in, too. The EMTs worked hard on George, taking turns to step in as the rhythmic thud of compressions echoed from the parked ambulance. The driver, usually relegated to the front, had abandoned the wheel to assist in the effort. "Breathe, George," coaxed one of the EMTs, as a defibrillator discharged.

But George apparently couldn't. The paramedics and EMTs exchanged glances. Minutes later, the paramedic on hand pulled a white sheet over George, spreading it gently over his face.

The picnic, naturally, broke up soon after. Solemn neighbors were about to collect their serving plates when blue lights indicated the arrival of the Sunset Ridge police force. The officers quickly moved in and asked everyone to leave their plates where they were.

An officer introduced himself to everyone as Detective Warren Watson. He was a tall man in early middle age with cropped dark hair. “What I’d like to do,” he said in a tone that brooked no argument, “is to speak with everybody before they leave. We’re going to take witness reports close to the road, away from the scene. Those of you with children will go first.”

It ended up being a fairly orderly process. The young moms and dads gave statements first.

“What’s going on?” Chad murmured to Samantha. “I thought people were saying it was a food allergy.”

Sam had been staring thoughtfully back at the picnic tables. “The police must need to check it all out. Just in case.”

Nora appeared like a wizened gnome at Sam’s elbow, making her jump. She was surveying the scene with some satisfaction. “This doesn’t surprise me at all.”

Chad quirked an eyebrow at Sam before saying in a genial tone, “It doesn’t?”

“Not a bit.” Nora frowned at Chad and grudgingly introduced herself. Chad gamely did the same. The formalities completed, Nora continued. “Nope. George was the kind of guy who everybody wanted to bump off.”

Chad seemed relieved that someone might have information about the incident. “You think he was murdered?”

Nora gave him a disappointed look, as if her suspicions of his dimness had been confirmed. "Naturally." She waved a hand toward the police cars, which still had their blue lights going.

"But why do you think that?" asked Chad curiously. "Wasn't it some sort of allergic reaction? More of a terrible accident? Maybe the police are simply doing their duty by checking it out."

Sam said quietly, "Because George brought his own food."

Nora turned sharply toward her, looking surprised, then grudgingly respectful. "That is correct," she said. "George always brought his own meals to neighborhood gatherings."

"But no EpiPen?" asked Sam.

Nora shrugged. "He clearly didn't think that was important, if he was eating food he prepared himself."

Chad gave a low whistle, looking grim. "So someone doctored his food. With . . . what was it he was allergic to?"

"Almonds."

Chad frowned. "Just almonds? Not peanuts or cashews?"

Nora gave him an annoyed look, as if he was being deliberately obtuse. "Just almonds. Sometimes people have allergies to only one kind of nut."

Sam had stopped listening to Nora and was gazing back toward the picnic tables again. Someone had gotten close enough to George Turner to put almonds on his plate. With thirty or more people around. And Nora, if memory served, had been one of them.

"What was he eating?" asked Sam. "It seems like he'd have been able to notice almonds in most foods."

Chad said, "Yeah, but people aren't looking at their food at a party. At least, I'm not. I'm looking at the people I'm talking with."

"Good point," said Sam. "But still, it would have been risky. The whole thing was risky—putting nuts in his meal with people around, then trusting George wouldn't see them and dump his plate in the trash."

"I have no idea what George was eating," said Nora.

"I know what he was eating," said Chad with a shrug. "It looked like some type of grain salad. Not rice. What's that other grain that people like in salads?"

"Quinoa," said Sam absently.

"That's it," said Chad. "Anyway, he seemed like a really interesting guy. He was telling me what he did for a living and stuff like that. Maybe he got too close to someone *else's* almond meal. You know? You hear about kids with peanut allergies, and the whole class can't eat peanut butter if the student is that sensitive."

Nora's expression showed that her opinion of Chad's intelligence hadn't improved. "I think it's a lot more likely that someone put almonds in his quinoa salad, don't you?"

"Who would want to kill George?" Chad asked, reasonably. "He seemed great."

Sam hadn't gotten that impression at all. But Chad often did look at life and people on the sunny side. Still, Sam wondered if maybe she'd made a snap judgment about George after his dismissal of her.

"You didn't know him," snapped Nora. "He was the kind of person who became more annoying as you became better acquainted."

Sam said, "Who found him the most annoying?"

"Everyone he came across," said Nora with yet another sniff.

Sam decided maybe she hadn't made a snap judgment on George after all.

"Specifically? It might be especially important so we can see if they're in attendance today," said Sam. "In fact, let's do this." She took her phone from the pocket of her dress and subtly took several pictures, documenting all the attendees.

Nora gave Sam that look of grudging respect again. "Well, there's George's son, of course. Mark? Marcus? Whatever. I know they got on each other's nerves all the time."

"You were friendly with George?" asked Chad, sounding surprised.

"Of course not!" barked Nora. "You haven't been paying attention."

Chad looked chastened. "It's just that I thought you must know George well if you were aware of his family dynamics."

"Not a bit. I simply happen to have lived next door to the man. It's impossible to avoid hearing arguments when they happen outside and right next to my house." Nora apparently didn't want to appear nosy.

"Which one is Marcus or Mark?" asked Sam.

"It's Marcus—I just remembered his name. He followed the ambulance. I suppose he'll be calling a funeral home. He's not here now, but I saw him earlier. Even said hello. You try to be friendly at these things. Anyway, George's son and he were like oil and water. The two of them bickered all the time."

"But Marcus attended the picnic," said Sam, frowning. "Why would he come? Does he live in the neighborhood?"

"Certainly not," said Nora. "Why would he want to live near a family member he doesn't get along with?"

It was a fair question. But it still didn't explain why Marcus, a non-resident, would attend a neighborhood picnic with a man he actively disliked.

Nora added, "His dad probably wanted him to come to the picnic to help him bring food or a chair or something. George was always asking Marcus to come over to lug things around or help him with trimming his bushes or some such."

Chad said, "I'm surprised Marcus would come help, considering he didn't like his dad much."

"Maybe he didn't like his dad, but he might have liked his dad's money. George had plenty of it. It could be that Marcus wanted to stay enough on George's good side so he wouldn't get written out of the will." Nora looked pleased at having come up with this idea.

"Marcus needed money?" asked Chad.

Nora scowled at him. "He's a doctor."

"So Marcus *doesn't* need money," said Chad wryly.

"Maybe he does," Sam said. "He couldn't be very old, if he's George's son. In his early thirties, maybe? He could have a lot of school loan debt to pay off." She smiled at Nora. "I knew you were an insider."

Nora puffed up a bit at the compliment.

Chad said, "Isn't it a little odd that Marcus didn't rush to help with the medical treatment of his father? Not that it was likely to do any good, I'm afraid."

Nora said, "That's exactly what I'm telling you. He wanted his father to croak."

Sam said mildly, "I was more under the impression that he was frozen. Or in shock."

"Whatever," said Nora airily. "Marcus isn't the only person with a tough relationship with George. There's also that woman right there."

Nora, who obviously wasn't shy about pointing, gestured to an attractive woman in her late-fifties with golden-brown hair. The woman was currently being interviewed by the police and seemed flushed and flustered.

"That's Julia Harper. She's had a long-standing feud with George. I'll certainly be filling the police in on *that*. I doubt anyone else will think of it."

Sam was about to press Nora for more information when a police officer strode up and indicated that he wanted to speak with Nora. Instead of looking the slightest bit dismayed, Nora seemed delighted. She gave Chad and Sam a quick wave and left with the police officer.

Before the two of them could comment on what they'd heard, another officer joined them to get statements.

Chad said, "Is this a suspicious death, officer?"

The officer gave him an inscrutable look. "This is routine. Now I'd like to start with getting your information."

They duly gave him their names and address. The policeman quirked an eyebrow. "Chad Fuller and Samantha Prescott? You're a couple?"

"We're married," said Sam. "I didn't take Chad's name for professional reasons."

"Okay. How well did you know George Turner?" asked the police officer. He had a suspicious look in his eyes as he looked at them. Fortunately, Sam had spotted that same expression on his face when he spoke to others. Otherwise, she'd be feeling quite paranoid by this point.

Chad quickly said, "We don't know *anyone* well. We moved to Maple Hills subdivision a few days ago. We were at the picnic primarily to meet everyone."

The policeman lifted an eyebrow. "You seemed chummy with the older woman you were speaking with."

Chad managed to look guilty even when he was completely innocent. He flushed. "We just met her. We were talking to her to pass the time until we gave our statement."

The officer reluctantly accepted this. He made a note on his notepad, and Chad gave Sam an anxious look.

"Did either of you speak with the deceased while you were at the picnic?"

Sam said, "I didn't have the chance." Although she'd wanted to.

Chad said, "He introduced himself, and we chatted for a while."

The officer made another note. "Did Mr. Turner seem preoccupied with anything? Distracted? Concerned about his safety?"

"Not a bit," said Chad. "He filled me in on what line of work he'd been in before he retired."

"He was retired?" asked the cop, checking his notes.

"Early, yes. He was only in his fifties. But it sounded like he was enjoying himself. He talked about his interest in woodworking and all the books he'd finally been able to catch up on."

The police officer was beginning to look bored. "No mention of any concerns. Any troubles."

Chad, always eager to help, thought carefully on this. "No," he finally said in a regretful voice. "Oh, he did say he was concerned that it might start raining before the end of the picnic. But that was the only worry he mentioned."

The cop pressed his lips together at this rather unhelpful concern expressed by George Turner. He turned to Samantha. His expression indicated that he expected her statement to be as pointless as her husband's had been.

He leaned forward, though, and started quickly scribbling notes as Sam said, "Well, first off, you'll want to know which plate is George Turner's. Fortunately, we were able to ascertain that information. My husband noticed he was eating quinoa."

Chad looked pleased to have contributed, despite not having offered the information himself.

"And which plate was that?" asked the officer.

"If I may?" asked Sam, gesturing toward the now-cordoned-off picnic area.

"You can't go in there, but if you can point toward it, that would help."

The three of them moved as closely as possible to the scene. Sam pointed out the plate. "Right there. We pushed it away from George because we were concerned the allergens were too close."

Another quirk of a brow. "Allergens?"

"Yes. According to a neighbor, George had a severe allergy to almonds and always brought his own food from home when he attended Maple Hills functions. I also saw it listed on his medical bracelet."

More scribbling by the officer. "Which neighbor was this?"

"Her name is Nora. She's the older woman you were mentioning earlier. One of the other officers spoke with her a minute ago." Sam waited until the officer finished scrawling. She smiled at him, a smile that was not returned. "I'm interested in hearing why the police are here. It does appear to be a suspicious death, but no one at the station would have known that."

The officer gave Sam a steady look. "It was very quiet at the station. When the call came through dispatch, we decided to come check it out."

Sam and Chad looked at each other. They weren't accustomed to places with quiet police stations. Charlotte's police departments had always seemed busy.

"You're free to go," said the policeman. "Thanks for your help."

They watched as he walked up to a group of cops to share what he knew.

Chapter Three

Samantha and Chad walked more slowly on their way back home than the brisk walk they'd made before arriving at the picnic.

"You didn't tell the officer the information about George's son," observed Chad slowly. "Or about the woman who George had a long-standing feud with."

Sam shrugged. "It was basically hearsay. For all I know, Nora made it up or has an overactive imagination. Besides, I wasn't about to steal her thunder. It was probably the highlight of Nora's week telling the police about all her suspicions related to George's death."

They started up the long driveway to the house. Chad had fallen in love with the place when they'd toured it with their agent, which had surprised Sam. She'd always thought Chad might be more drawn to starkly modern homes with recent updates. The brick house had a rather stately façade with columns, arched windows, cornices, and moldings, and a wide veranda. A wrought-iron fence surrounded the property.

Sam said, "What was George like?"

"Seemed like a great guy."

Sam gave a wry smile. After ten-plus years with Chad, she was used to his positive views on most people. "I remember your mentioning that. You said he talked a little about what he'd done for a living before he retired early."

"Oh, right. Yes, I had the feeling George was happy to relive his glory days in property development. He created residential communities and commercial complexes."

"Sounds exciting," said Sam dryly.

"Well, it wasn't *riveting* conversation, but he told a good story. He was talking about incorporating green spaces and sustainable design practices."

Sam asked, "Did you get any sort of sense of what he was like as a person? Right now, he sounds like just some sort of corporate entity."

Chad considered this. "I'd say he was your typical successful businessman. Assertive, confident. He seemed like he was very involved in the community, both in Maple Hills but also in the greater Sunset Ridge area."

"Hmm. I wonder if that was what made people dislike him so much." Sam took out her key from her dress pocket and unlocked the heavy front door.

"What do you mean?" Chad flopped down in an armchair.

"If George was so used to being in charge all the time, he probably wasn't the easiest person to deal with when it came to processing HOA requests. Right? He sounds like someone who was accustomed to control."

Chad lifted his eyebrows. "You think one of our neighbors killed him for denying their request to build a fence?"

"Maybe. Murder happens for all sorts of petty reasons, doesn't it? We read about that kind of stuff in the paper all the time. At any rate, it *had* to be a neighbor. Unless we think someone outside Maple Hills broke into George's house, tampered with his quinoa salad, and then escaped."

"Sounds unlikely," admitted Chad. He gave a yawn. "Suddenly, I'm totally exhausted. That picnic ended up being a lot more stressful than I thought it was going to be. I figured it would be bad enough just meeting people, smiling a lot, and trying to eat and talk at the same time. Having murder thrown into the equation was more than I expected." He glanced over at his wife. "Want to take a nap?"

Sam couldn't be less interested in napping. Instead of feeling tired from the catastrophic picnic, she felt energized. "I'm all hyped up, sorry."

Chad didn't look surprised. Samantha was almost always on the go. "I guess that probably came with the territory."

"The territory?" asked Sam as she picked up her notebook from a side table.

"Yes. The fact you had to leap into battle to direct everyone, then try to help George. Your adrenalin was pumping. It's a good thing you were there. Everybody else was staring at him, not sure what to do, including me. They should make an action figure out of you."

Sam made a face. "I don't know about that. The action figure would have to have its batteries replaced all the time."

"Do action figures have batteries?" Chad tilted his head to one side. "Not so sure about that. Okay, I'm off for a nap. Wake me up if you need me for anything." He headed off for the stairs.

Sam settled in the armchair Chad had vacated with her notebook. Lists were always a helpful way for her to calm down. She'd tried almost about every way possible to make a list. She'd tinkered with list-making apps on her phone and created them with Word documents. But lately, she'd appreciated the old-school method of pen and paper. There was something uniquely satisfying about striking things off the list.

This new list, however, would not be one of her regular, to-do varieties. It was going to be a list of what she knew. George Turner, despite his questionable personality, had certainly not deserved to die in his neighborhood at a picnic he likely helped organize. Having been right on the scene as George breathed his last, Samantha felt a personal obligation to lend her organizational skills to help figure out who might have prematurely ended his life.

She wrote:

1. *Nora. Older neighbor, rather crotchety. Seemed very satisfied to see that George was dead. Issues with the HOA? Nora mentioned that she'd tried to start a neighborhood watch, and George had shut her down.*
2. *Marcus. George's son. Nora lived next door to George and noticed some arguments between the two men. Marcus was at the picnic—why? Nora thought Marcus tried to stay in George's good graces because George had a lot of money. But Marcus is a physician. Was Marcus trying to make his father happy by being there, or was he at the picnic for another reason? He should have had plenty of opportunity to tamper with George's food, since*

he would naturally have been standing with his father at least sometimes. And he was frozen when his father went into shock.

3. *Julia Harper. Nora said she and George had some sort of long-standing feud. What was the feud over? Did anyone see her close to George's plate before Chad and I arrived at the picnic?*
4. *Who was that woman who shrank back and looked alarmed when George approached her?*

Sam sat back, re-reading what she'd written. Then she bobbed her head, satisfied. It was a start. She stood up, looking around her house for something to tackle. The problem with being over-organized, however, is there often isn't anything for you to do. Sam didn't feel much like mopping the floor, which she supposed was the next thing to be done. Instead, she decided on a brisk walk around the neighborhood. Not only would it relieve some of her pent-up energy, it might offer the opportunity to get neighbors' reactions to the picnic. Although she didn't think she wanted to speak with Nora Snodwick again today. She'd had quite enough Nora for the day.

Sam headed to the bedroom to change her clothes, thinking a yellow dress was a bit too much for a walk around the neighborhood. She expected to see Chad snoring away, but he was lying on the bed, looking at his phone.

He yawned again when he saw her. "Hey there. Decided to go to sleep, after all?"

"No, I thought a walk might do me good. I thought you were going to nap."

Chad gave her a rueful look. “My body tells me I’m worn out, but my brain is still too busy to shut down. Maybe I’ll finally knock off by the time you get back from your walk.”

“Want to come along?” she asked as she pulled on athletic shorts and a tee-shirt.

“Nope! That’s all you. I definitely don’t have the energy to handle a walk. Especially the way *you* walk.”

Sam frowned. “I wasn’t aware I walked in a difficult way.”

“Fast. You walk fast. I have to scramble to keep up. No, I’ll lazily scroll through social media, thank you very much. By the time you return, I’ll probably have bored myself into dozing.”

A minute later, Sam let herself out the front door, pocketing the key. She surveyed the route options from the veranda. The house was at the top of the subdivision, giving her a good view of many of the roads. There was a nice loop she could take to return home without turning around. She pulled out her phone and checked the GPS. Actually, there were two different options for looped walks. Choosing the longer one, she set out.

Sam was hoping to see neighbors visiting over fences or by their mailboxes. But Maple Hills was sadly rather quiet, currently. Maybe the horrible events at the picnic had made everybody just as exhausted as Chad had been. She passed a variety of different houses, some small, some larger, some older, some newer. When they’d toured the new house and the neighborhood, they’d both liked the idea of being in a place with different people from different income levels and backgrounds.

After ten minutes of walking, Sam’s ears perked up at the sound of activity ahead. She hoped she wouldn’t be disappointed to learn it was someone’s yard service. Sam walked even more briskly to see it was the woman Nora identified as Julia Harper, the one who allegedly had a long-standing feud with George.

Julia might have been in the same over-stimulated state that Sam was in. She was attacking her front yard with verve, flinging weeds everywhere. She'd looked very stylish and reserved at the picnic, but here in her yard, wearing old clothes, she looked like a completely different person. But she still retained that elegant look somehow, with her high cheekbones and slender form.

Julia didn't look particularly delighted when she spotted Sam walking toward her. She attempted to smooth down her hair, which was standing out from her head in different directions. Apparently deciding it was futile, she gave Sam a somewhat welcoming smile, although her eyes were wary.

"You're the new neighbor, aren't you?" she asked. She removed a gardening glove and extended it to Sam.

"Samantha, yes. People usually call me Sam."

"Good to meet you. I'm Julia Harper."

Sam said, "How about if I help you out here? Weeding can be kind of cathartic, can't it?"

Julia quirked a brow. "You must have witnessed my exuberant weed tossing."

"It was very impressive."

Julia gritted her teeth into a smile. "I appreciate it, but I'll keep pick up with it again in a little while. I can use the exercise, as well as the stress-relief. What a welcome to the neighborhood, hmm?"

"Oh, you mean the picnic? Well, it was very sad, wasn't it?"

Julia looked as if she might have described it with a different word. "I'm sorry that was your introduction to Maple Hills. I promise there aren't usually medical emergencies at our subdivision events."

"I didn't even have the chance to meet him. George, I mean. He was the homeowner association president, wasn't he?"

Julia took off her other gardening glove, tossing both casually near a pile of pulled weeds. "He was indeed. I think your husband met him, though, right?" She gave Sam a look through narrowed eyes.

"He sure did. He thought he was a great guy."

Julia's mouth twisted a little. "Sounds like George was putting his best foot forward for the new folks." She seemed to be trying to decide something before giving a small shrug. "Would you like to come inside? I can only be so hospitable out here in the yard."

"I don't want to be any bother," said Sam, but she was already moving toward the house.

Julia's house was made of stone and was as elegant as she was. The interior was full of modern, Swedish-looking furniture, lending the design a very minimalist quality. She gestured absently to a chair. "Take a seat." She paused, then said, "I hope this won't permanently ruin your opinion of me, but I could frankly use a drink after that picnic. Would you like one?"

Sam considered this. One of her personal standards was that she never drank before five, nor after six-fifteen. This was decidedly out of her window. However, she did want to talk to Julia, who was looking at her with an impatient expression on her face.

"Sure," she said, hoping she sounded breezy. "A glass of wine would be great, thank you."

Julia quirked an eyebrow at her and pulled out a dusty bottle of red wine from the depths of a cabinet. After pouring a glass for Sam, she grabbed a decidedly non-dusty bottle of bourbon and poured herself a large amount, putting a splash of ginger ale in there for good measure.

While Julia was playing bartender, Sam glanced around the living room. There was absolutely nothing to indicate anything personal about Julia. The artwork seemed to have been selected to coordinate with the white Swedish furniture. There were no photographs. No clutter. No dust, aside from that spotted on the unpopular bottle of wine. From her observations, Sam concluded Julia was likely as Type-A as she was. It took one to know one.

Julia took a slug from her glass. "So, tell me about the house. Are you fixing it up? Did it *need* to be fixed up? All the neighbors are dying to know. If I get the scoop, I'll be in real demand."

"Didn't the previous owners have everybody over?"

Julia snorted. "Never. They acted more like lords of the manor. They didn't exactly want to mix with the peasants."

Sam sighed a little. It sounded like she might have some damage control to handle. Even though people knew there were *new* neighbors, the irritation with the old neighbors might take a while to dissolve. "To answer your question," Sam said brightly, "the house was basically move-in ready. Come over anytime. In fact, I may have to host a gathering at our house so everyone can check out the inside."

"Then *you'll* be in real demand. That'll be one hot ticket. It's just that it's a historical home and seems really cool from the outside."

Sam nodded. "It's pretty cool from the inside, too. I'll definitely make a note to have a get-together."

"But you just moved in. I'd think that would be headache enough for the time being. Do it for Christmas and give yourself a few months to get settled." Julia took another gulp of the bourbon and ginger ale.

"Everything is actually already put away. We're settled."

Julia raised her glass in an admiring toast. "I can tell we have a lot in common. Tell me a little about the two of you. What do you do?"

Sam gave another small sigh. She's tried, over time, to finesse this, but it never seemed to sound better. Somehow, no matter how she phrased things, she and Chad always sounded like a couple of bums.

"Well, I'm not really working now, except in the volunteer sector. I'm going to be looking for local opportunities to help."

Sam could tell Julia was mentally calculating the cost of the large historic home she and Chad had purchased. "And Chad?"

"Oh, he sometimes does contract jobs for financial companies. Mostly, he's pretty free, too."

Julia's lips quirked into a half-smile. "Okay, so there's a story there, clearly. I've had enough to drink to be nosy. There's some money somewhere, right?"

Sam felt her face flushing. She said brusquely, "There was an app."

"An app?"

Sam nodded. "That's right. Just a thing. Nothing important, just something fairly useful for businesses that needed project collaboration and management. I invented the app, introducing an AI component, then I sold it. Some money was generated from that sale."

"I'd say," said Julia with a low whistle. "Heavens." She took another sip of her drink. "So, did the two of you have a local move? From one neighborhood in Sunset Ridge to another?"

"No, we actually made the move from Charlotte. We had a moving company to help us, although we ended up packing a bunch of fragile items in our cars." She smiled. "It was a pity Chad had downsized to a smaller, less-expensive car before the move. A hybrid. His Range Rover would have probably been helpful."

"What made you decide to move here?" asked Julia.

"We've always loved the mountains and liked the idea of moving to a smaller town. Traffic was getting pretty hectic in Charlotte."

"So you're not from around here?" Julia frowned.

Sam suppressed a sigh. She'd been warned by a well-meaning postal worker that residents of Sunset Ridge had gotten fairly territorial over their town and weren't delighted by newcomers, even those from the same state. She hadn't experienced that yet, but felt as if she just had. "No, we're all new here," she said brightly.

Julia frowned again, not saying anything.

Sam hurried on. "Anyway, that's the story with us. But I'm a lot more interested in what happened to George Turner this afternoon."

"Well, we all knew he had a food allergy. I guess someone forgot and put nuts in something. George must not have been paying close attention and ate whatever it was." Julia shrugged a thin shoulder. "It's a tragic accident." Something in her expression, though, made Sam doubt Julia believed her own words.

Sam said, "That's what I'd heard, too, about the food allergy. The only problem, though, is that George apparently always brought his own food to neighborhood events. He was supposedly pretty diligent about it."

A flash of irritation crossed Julia's features. "So George sampled something from the potluck. Everybody has days where they're not totally thinking straight."

"Agreed. Although the police seemed very interested in the alternate explanation." Sam was engaging in a bit of hyperbole with that statement. The police had, instead, seemed mostly bored and as if they were looking for drama to stir up.

"What's the alternate explanation?"

Sam said, "That George was deliberately given the almonds by someone around him. Someone who slipped the nuts into his salad."

Julia frowned. "Murder, you mean."

Sam nodded again.

"Wouldn't that have been an absolutely insane thing to do? There were thirty-odd people grouped tightly together." Julia knocked back the remaining bit of alcohol, then stood and staggered for a refill. "More for you?" she asked in an attempt at good hostessing.

"I'm fine, thanks. And yes, it would have been risky, from the murderer's point-of-view, but think how these gatherings usually are. People are trying to give others good impressions of themselves. They're trying to contribute to the conversation.

They're probably not paying a lot of attention to what's going on around them."

Julia returned with her glass and sat quietly for a few moments. "I guess I didn't really think about the cops being there. I was startled when they wanted to speak with everyone, but I didn't think it through. Maybe I didn't *want* to think it through. That means that someone in Maple Hills, someone I know, is a killer." She took a large sip of her drink. "When the officer was asking me questions, I was pretty indignant about it. I mean, I wasn't standing anywhere close to George at the picnic. I was trying, as usual, to avoid him."

"Were you?"

"Naturally. To know George was to want to avoid George." Julia gave a chuckle. "Anyway, I don't know how the cops expected anybody to give a great alibi. I doubt anyone really remembered where anyone else was standing, who they spoke with, or what they said. It's just something you *go* to, right? A neighborhood picnic that you feel you need to attend."

Sam said, "So you weren't George's biggest fan?"

"Nope. Nobody was. I haven't spoken to him for a while, since I was doing so well with my goal of avoiding him at all costs. Frankly, I'm not at all sorry that he's gone, although I had nothing to do with his death . . . accident or not. I'd like to throw a party for whoever did, though."

Sam gave Julia a smile. "So, like you said earlier, it sounds like there's a story there."

"Yes, I guess there is. I'm an architect, although I'm taking on fewer jobs now than I used to. George was a developer. George retired early and I've been slowing down, myself. Like yourself, we were looking for ways to volunteer our skills to the community for various projects."

Sam asked, "You and George served on a project together?"

"That's right. It was a park revitalization for Sunset Ridge Park. The goal was to create a more vibrant and attractive space for residents to enjoy. George stepped up to lead the project. Naturally. I was the project designer. I also have an interest in landscaping, although you'd never know that from all the weeds I yanked up outside today." She gave a dry, somewhat tipsy laugh. "My job was not only developing the park's design, but selecting plants for the project."

"That's a huge role," said Sam. "I'm surprised the city didn't hire you for that instead of having it be a volunteer position."

"Yeah, well, Sunset Ridge is always looking for ways to save a buck. Once they had an architect onboard, I guess they figured there was no point in spending any money to hire somebody officially."

Sam said, "With George as the project lead, I'm thinking you might have butted heads with him during the process."

"That's putting it mildly. He was on a total power trip through the whole thing. You'd think he'd be trying to put the good of the community first and himself second, but that's not the way it played out. As the lead, he was in charge of budget allocation, working with the local government, securing grants, and managing funds. And he was in constant conflict with me over every little thing. He didn't like the playground design I'd come up with. He disagreed with the figures I'd given him, even though they were well within the budget the city set."

Sam made a face. "Sounds like he was determined to sabotage you."

"Exactly. To make matters worse, the issues seeped over into Maple Hills. I'd propose something at the annual HOA meeting and somehow George and I would end up in a shouting match. It made everyone uncomfortable, of course. I started withdrawing from all the different subdivision events because I wanted to avoid George and the clashes that would inevitably ensue. It was causing me a lot of strain."

Sam nodded. "Of course it would. It's one thing to have it happen outside Maple Hills, but it's something else to have it impact your daily life in the neighborhood."

"He was ugly to me. I'd be taking a walk or doing yardwork and he'd drive by and make rude gestures. When I wanted to put solar panels on my roof, George rejected my request outright, even though the HOA had approved others here."

"He sounds like a real charmer," said Sam. George had clearly been trying to make a good impression when he spoke with Chad. Of course, Chad sometimes wasn't the most perceptive of men.

"It was becoming incredibly stressful for me to live here. I was seriously thinking about putting my house on the market and moving somewhere else. But then I'd realize that meant George would have won. He'd probably have thrown a party to celebrate when my house went up for sale. So I stayed put. And it's a good thing I did, because now my problem is taken care of."

Sam said, "You must be feeling a lot more relaxed."

"Well, relaxed enough to spend time in my front yard," said Julia wryly. "I'd been avoiding being out there, and the weeds went berserk." She frowned, rubbing her forehead. "But now I have other worries. The busybodies in this neighborhood will fill the police in on my squabble with George. I must be looking like suspect number one." She sounded annoyed, but also slightly amused by the idea.

"George sounds like the type of person who probably had plenty of folks angry with him. I wouldn't worry too much about it," said Sam. She paused. In a deceptively idle voice she said, "Who's in charge of the homeowner association now?"

"Hmm? Oh, I suppose the vice president steps in. He's this ghastly man named Hank. It's a testament to George's horribleness that Hank will seem like an improvement." Julia rubbed her head again. "Or maybe the presidency goes up for election. Honestly, I have no idea. I suppose it's in the HOA bylaws."

"Do you have them? The bylaws? I don't have a copy of them."

Julia raised an eyebrow at Sam's eagerness. "My, my! Are you interested in running for HOA president?"

"Are you?" asked Sam, not particularly wanting to step on any toes at this early stage.

"No way. George poisoned me against HOA involvement for life. I'm planning on sending in my proxy votes and skipping the meetings altogether. The meetings were always too contentious for me, anyway. It's aggravating, too, having to scrape and bow in front of a committee to get something done on your own property. It's a pity we have to have an HOA at all. It's only good to keep folks from painting their houses chartreuse or from having chickens running around people's front yards. No, the presidency is not for me. But you? You'd make a fine president, I believe."

Sam gave a little sigh. "Contentious? I'm sorry to hear that."

"Well, it's to be expected, I suppose, when you have people like George and Hank who love wielding power and telling everyone no. Hank is something of a bully and really enjoys getting his own way. George was . . . well, he was George."

Sam said, "Okay. Well, if you could email me those bylaws, I'll take a look. I'd love to hop in and help."

"You'd surely be a lot more reasonable than any of the alternatives." Julia looked sadly into her empty cup. "Going back to George's death, I surely hope the police find a better candidate than me for a suspect."

"Do you have any thoughts about who might be?"

Julia considered this. She opened her mouth slowly, then snapped it back shut again as if she'd reconsidered her words. Finally, she said, "I don't know anything for certain, of course. But if I had to pick somebody, I'm thinking it might be Pris Lawrence."

"I haven't met Pris yet."

Julia said, "You'll know who I'm talking about. She's the one who was standing on the fringes of the picnic, looking anxious."

Sam remembered the woman in her 30s with the jet-black hair. "Yes, I remember her. I was wondering why she was sticking to the perimeter."

Julia shrugged. "She's a strange creature. She was probably poised for flight. If she was on the edges, she could bolt back home quickly. The woman is a recluse. I mean, *I* was trying to keep from leaving the house to avoid George, but Pris takes things to a whole new level. She's a real oddity."

"Is there something wrong? Does she have agoraphobia?"

"Who knows?" said Julia in a bored tone. "She's always like that."

"Have you seen her often?"

"Nope," said Julia. "She shies away from the Maple Ridge gatherings. I was shocked she was at the picnic."

Sam knit her brows. "That does seem out of character, if she usually avoids the events. Maybe she has social anxiety."

Julia shrugged. "Then why go to a picnic when the entire neighborhood is there?"

"I think people with social anxiety often *want* to be part of the group. It's just very challenging. Maybe she thought she could hang out at the picnic for a little while, talk to a couple of people, then go back home."

"In that case, it was a total failure," said Julia dryly. "She's absolutely the unfriendliest neighbor in Maple Hills."

Sam wondered if it was the alcohol talking. Being shy wasn't the same thing as being unfriendly. Her heart went out to Pris a little.

Julia waved her empty cup at Sam. "Want another glass?"

Sam hadn't finished the glass of red that Julia had given her. "No, I'm all right. I should leave you to it."

Julia heaved a sigh. "Back to the weeding, then. Somehow it seems like a less-attractive activity now that I've had a break from it. Well, thanks for coming by. If you visit again, we won't talk about murder the whole time."

"Sounds like a plan," said Sam lightly.

"And I'll send you those HOA bylaws. George should have provided those to you from the start."

Chapter Four

The next morning, Sam composed an email to Hank, the homeowner association vice president. She'd carefully read the bylaws that Julia had sent her way and had found that an election needed to be called to fill the empty position. She told Hank she was interested in running.

She waited for five minutes for a response. Sometimes she communicated with people who had email open all the time. Rather disappointingly, Hank didn't seem to be one of those people. She closed her laptop as Chad came into the sunroom.

"Everything okay?" he asked. He'd just woken up and his hair was sticking up in all different directions on his head.

"It's good. I'm running for HOA president, like we talked about."

"Oh, okay," said Chad. "So the bylaws said another election had to be held?"

"That's right. I emailed Hank, the vice president, and asked him to list me as a candidate."

Chad quirked an eyebrow. "Do we think Hank is going to run for the spot himself?"

"Probably. He sounds like a power-hungry type, from what I gathered from Julia yesterday. A bully, I think she said." Sam checked emails on her phone. "No reply from Hank yet."

"It's Sunday morning," said Chad dryly. "He's probably pouring himself a cup of coffee before discovering his dreams of HOA control are about to be dashed." He paused. "You know I believe in you one-hundred percent. You're always able to make things happen and get things done. But no one in this neighborhood even knows you. Are you sure that you're going to get votes?"

"Well, I figured one of two things will happen. Either Hank and I will be the only ones on the ballot, and I win because everyone dislikes Hank. Or, I'll win because I've knocked on everyone's door and put signs up."

Chad grinned at her. "Why do I have the feeling that option two is going to happen, regardless of whether there are more than two people on the ballot?"

"Because it's the smart thing to do?" Sam said, smiling back at him. "I'm going to have signs made up with a picture of me on them and my phone number. And I'm going on a listening tour this afternoon to find out what people like about Maple Hills and the HOA, and what people don't."

"I predict you'll win the office of president, hands-down." Chad poured himself a large cup of coffee. "What can I do to help?"

Sam didn't particularly want Chad to go on the listening tour with her. He was a charming conversationalist, but he was apt to go off on tangents. She wanted her visits to be brief and focused. But Chad might need a mission to keep him occupied.

"How about if you dig up a decent picture of me on the computer? Then maybe you can help me put up signs once they're made."

"Sure," said Chad. "How long will that be?"

"I looked online, and it's apparently a 24-hour turnaround."

Chad smiled at her. "You have the presidency in the bag, you know."

"Well, considering how much energy I'm planning on throwing at it, let's hope so. I'll be pretty devastated if it doesn't work out."

"Don't worry. They'll be relieved to have someone new to vote for after all the issues people have had with the HOA in the past. Where are you starting out with your listening tour?"

Sam, actually, knew exactly where she was planning on starting out. When she'd finished up her walk yesterday, she'd seen the woman who'd shrunk back from George at the picnic, leaving her house and getting into her car. Sam was very curious to find out why she'd been afraid of George. But this seemed all too complicated to share with Chad, plus there was always the very real concern he might try to stop her from questioning potential murderers. It certainly seemed that the woman might qualify as a suspect, given her visceral reaction to George. "Oh, I'll probably start out with our closer neighbors and fan out from there. I won't be able to do it all this afternoon, of course."

Actually, Sam hoped very much that she *would* be able to do it all this Sunday afternoon. But she knew that being overly ambitious was setting herself up for failure. A neighbor could end up being particularly chatty. Others might not answer the door at all. Which reminded her of something else.

"I should mark which houses I was able to speak with someone and which I need to return to." Sam frowned. "But we haven't gotten a map of the neighborhood, or even a directory."

"Which I'm sure wouldn't happen under a Samantha presidency." Chad started rummaging in the fridge for something to eat.

"I guess George was the one who'd send the packet of information to the new owners."

Chad peered into the fridge as if looking for inspiration. He said in a distracted tone. "Or else someone is falling down on the job."

"I guess I could ask Julia to forward over those other items. She got her hands on the bylaws easily enough."

"Do you have her contact information?" asked Chad.

"No. I should have asked for it," said Sam, feeling very irritated with herself for the lapse. She'd clearly been too involved in thinking about the murder. "I only have her email address, and who knows how often she checks it?"

"Just run down there in the car and ask her in person. Although maybe you should wait for a more appropriate time. Since it's Sunday morning." Chad stressed this again, knowing that Sam had been up since 5:30 and it likely felt like the middle of the day to her.

"It's all very annoying," said Sam. Now she was going to have to think of a project of some kind to stall with until it was later in the day. She supposed she could always do yardwork. They employed a well-reviewed company to handle it, but there were still roses to be dead-headed, bushes to be trimmed, and likely things to be pulled. She simply might not approach the task with as much vigor as Julia had the day before. Sam thought it appeared Julia was trying to exorcize some personal demons in her wild weeding. She definitely wasn't too upset that George had perished at the picnic mere hours before.

"We could watch a movie," suggested Chad. "That would kill time."

But killing time was anathema to Sam. She was much more interested in being productive.

Chad said wryly, "Or not."

"Sorry. I just know I wouldn't be able to sit still during a movie."

"Brunch? We could go get something to eat." He shot a morose look at the fridge, apparently not having found anything appealing in its depths.

Sam realized she hadn't had anything to eat since 5:30 but a dairy-free yogurt with blueberries. "Actually, that might not be a bad idea."

Chad looked delighted that one of his suggestions was actually taken up on. "I'll grab my wallet."

An hour and a half later, after a leisurely brunch of shrimp and grits in downtown Sunset Ridge, Chad, and Sam drove back up their long driveway. "That was very tasty," said Chad. "But sadly, now I need a nap."

Sam, however, was quite alert. She'd had a coffee with a couple of refills at the restaurant and felt as if she was ready to take on the world.

"And I suppose you're heading out," said Chad with a grin. "I'd have thought you'd suffered a minor stroke if you decided to take a nap, too."

"Far too much coffee for that," said Sam cheerfully. She looked down at her outfit, which was a casual sundress. She stepped into the bathroom to apply the barest hint of pink lipstick, then reapplied mascara.

Sam hopped into the car and headed to Julia's house. Julia answered the door, looking dressed up in black slacks and a white button-down top. She gave Sam a half-smile. "Looking for more red wine?"

Sam chuckled. "No, not today. I wanted to thank you for the bylaws you sent over to me."

"What did you find out? I had the best intentions of looking up whether an election would need to be held, but I saw how boring and obtuse the text was and forwarded it over to you."

"We do need to have an election, apparently in the next week," said Sam.

"Really? That's soon, isn't it?"

Sam said, "I guess it's meant to keep the position from being empty while neighbors are waiting for their architectural review requests to be reviewed."

"Ah, makes sense. So you're running?"

"I am," said Sam pleasantly. "But I was wondering if I could trouble you about something else in the meantime. Could you forward me over a Maple Hills directory?"

"I can do better than that. I'll send you the Maple Hills directory *and* a map of the neighborhood."

"Perfect!" Sam said. "That's really helpful. I'm about to embark on a listening tour of the neighborhood, and I wanted to note which residents I'd spoken with and which I'd missed."

"Wow, you're really taking this seriously."

Sam shrugged. "I figured if I was going to run, I might as well make an effort to win. Otherwise, it's a waste of time, isn't it?"

Julia sent the information over, Sam said goodbye, then she headed back home to print the pages Julia had sent. Putting the sheets in a leather-bound notebook, Sam set off again, this time on foot.

No one answered at the first couple of houses she visited, which was most disappointing. One house might not have had anyone at home. The other, though, had two cars in the driveway. Sam hoped she didn't look like a door-to-door salesperson.

The door opened at the third house. Sam gave the man and woman a warm smile and introduced herself.

"Oh, you must be one of the new neighbors," said a woman who introduced herself as Mandy. She was a pleasant-looking woman of about forty with a broad face and curly hair in ringlets. She blushed. "I was planning on coming by with a welcome gift, but time slipped away from me.

Sam waved her hand to indicate that Mandy's concern was completely unnecessary. "No worries about that. Life gets really busy sometimes, doesn't it?"

Her husband, who said he was Alfred, was a gruff, bearded, burly man with a flushed face. "I'll say. Hectic is more the word for it. Mandy and I have been struggling lately finding time to do much of anything."

Sam beamed at them. "Well, maybe I can help. One reason I've dropped by this afternoon is because I'm running for HOA president. It might seem rather indelicate to do this so soon after George Turner's very unfortunate death, but the bylaws state that an election must be managed within a week of a vacated position."

"Mercy," said Mandy mildly.

Alfred said, "Well, it wasn't right, what happened to him. Although I can't say I ever warmed to the man."

"Alfred," remonstrated Mandy in a gentle voice.

"Sorry, but I didn't."

Mandy quickly said, "Gracious, where are my manners? Won't you come inside?"

Sam hesitated. She'd planned on having her listening tour be a doorstop tour. Going inside everyone's house would take significantly longer, and she didn't have that much time. There was something very appealing about Mandy and Alfred though. "Maybe just for a minute? I didn't mean to disturb you on your Sunday afternoon."

"No bother at all," said Alfred, holding the door open wide.

Their small home was cozy with colorful throws on the backs of sofas and armchairs. A chubby cat lifted its head to survey the visitor before dropping it again and curling up into a fluffy ball in an equally fluffy bed. There appeared to be a lot of paperwork and notebooks out, which Mandy clucked over, and cleared away so that she and Alfred could sit on the sofa across from the armchair they put Sam in.

"Those papers are spawning, I swear they are," said Alfred gloomily.

"Now Alfred, we don't want to bother Sam with our problems."

Sam sat up straight, eager to make the point. "Actually, that's exactly why I'm here today. I wanted to reach out to my new neighbors and listen to them. Find out what troubles them—not only about Maple Hills, but in general. I'd love to help if I can. To me, that's what being an HOA president is all about. I want to earn my votes."

Alfred and Mandy gave her a pitying look. "Heavens, that sounds like a nightmare," said Mandy. "You'll get an earful, I'm sure."

Alfred nodded, looking skeptical. "I know you've got good intentions. But you'll be opening up a can of worms like you've never seen before. People here go on and on about things. I swear it's a real talkative place. You'll never get any work done."

Sam smiled brightly, "That would be fine, because the only work I do is volunteer work. And I do really want to help."

Mandy and Alfred exchanged a look. Mandy said slowly, "Well, what's troubling us are these notices from the doctor's office. I had to take Alfred in recently when a cold he got turned into pneumonia."

"Funny how that can happen," mused Alfred, stroking his beard. "Just a regular, ordinary cold. Then a nasty cough. Then bronchitis."

"Then pneumonia," said Mandy with a sigh. "And I can tell you that getting this man to go to the doctor was a huge feat in itself."

Alfred gave a throaty laugh. "But I was right, wasn't I? It ended up causing a lot of bother."

Mandy leaned forward confidingly. "We got a fairly large bill. We hadn't met our deductible yet, you see."

"I bet we have now," said Alfred.

"Then, apparently, the doctor's office was in the middle of being merged with some big hospital system. We paid the bill, but when they were switching the computer systems from the one office to the hospital system, the record of the payment got lost."

Alfred offered helpfully, "A software migration, they called it."

"Anyway, the long and the short of it is that we couldn't get a representative over there," said Mandy. "We do both work, and out of the house. We'd both try before we went to work and during our lunch hours. We couldn't step away any longer than that. And we work past five o'clock, which is when the representatives stop taking phone calls."

Alfred said, "One time I was on hold my entire lunch hour. Then, the call dropped." He shook his head.

Mandy added, "Whenever we get somebody, they tell us we have to call the other place. So if we call the number for our doctor's office, they tell us the hospital system is handling the billing. If we call the hospital's number, they tell us Alfred's visit was before the merger and the doctor's office has to handle it."

"The runaround," said Alfred morosely. "We're getting the runaround."

"Worst of all, they sent it to collections for being unpaid. Now neither place will speak with us because they say only collections can legally talk to us about billing. But we paid it!"

This was precisely the kind of pointless problem that aggravated Sam the most. The kind of problem that made her want to rush in and fix everything. She said, "I know we just met, but this type of thing is what I'm great at helping with. If you'll trust me with the paperwork and you don't mind me handling it on your behalf, I'd be happy to take it on for you. I can call all different hours of the day."

"They won't talk to you, though, will they?" asked Mandy worriedly. "Because of the hippo thing."

"HIPAA," clarified Alfred.

This was true. Because of privacy concerns, they'd only speak to Samantha if she had a POA. Which, clearly, she didn't.

Alfred said slowly, "Mandy, how about if she pretended to be you? Just for this issue. They wouldn't know any better. And we do need to put this problem to rest. You haven't been able to sleep since this mess started."

"You haven't been much better," said Mandy. She turned to Sam, a hopeful expression on her face. "It's true—this has been worrying me sick. Would you mind taking over? I'll give you our birthdates, our address, the last four of our socials. That's all the stuff they usually ask to identify a person, right?"

Sam nodded. "That's it, I think. And the paperwork—whatever records you have, proof of payment, all of that."

Mandy and Alfred gave each other another look before quickly gathering up the paperwork and jotting down their identifying information for the calls. They put it all in a tote bag and handed it to Sam.

"I'd say you have our vote," said Alfred fervently.

Mandy said, "Now, if anything comes up, promise us that you won't worry with this anymore. Just return it, and we'll completely understand."

"Of course we will," said Alfred. "We're at the point of pulling our hair out, ourselves, so I can't imagine how you'll feel."

Sam stood up, giving them a bright smile. "I'll start right in on it tomorrow. And I'll let you know what kind of progress I'm able to make. Your cell numbers are in the directory, right?"

The two nodded. "Thank you," they chorused.

Sam gave them a wave and headed on her way.

Chapter Five

Sam considered heading home to drop off the tote bag, but found it lightweight and easy to carry. So she continued on her way. At the next few houses, the neighbors opened their doors and spoke with her on the doorstep, which was good news for the length of her listening tour. They told her all the things they wished Maple Hills would do differently. One couple wanted streetlights for nighttime strolls. One wanted more neighborhood events.

One complained about the barking of a dog a few doors down. The neighbor, an older woman with gray-streaked dark hair, said in a tired voice, "The barking is constant. But the real problem is that I just feel so darn bad about the poor little beast. Chained up every day, in the heat of summer and the dead of winter. Awful. Why even have a pet if you're going to do it that way? And the animal has such a sweet face. No wonder it's barking all the time."

Sam's radar went up again. "How long has the dog been chained up?"

"Since they got it. Years. It's a terrible life."

Sam frowned. "Surely that's against the law."

"If it's not, it should be. We all talk about it and how miserable it is," she said darkly. "I always think about running over there and kidnapping the poor baby."

The very thought had crossed Sam's mind, too.

After visiting several more houses and logging more data in terms of what her neighbors would like changed about Maple Hills, Sam came upon a small home with a small yard. Inside the yard was a small dog of indeterminate heritage whose tail started thumping against the ground as soon as he saw her. The little guy was irresistibly and appealingly ugly with large, soulful eyes. Sam suspected he might possess some basset hound with a pinch of cavalier king Charles spaniel thrown in. And perhaps a motley assortment of other breeds, as well. As reported, he was on a chain. And, despite the warmth of the day, appeared to have no water anywhere in sight.

Sam took a deep breath. Her first instinct was to take the dog off the chain, bring him home, and dote on him. This, however, was probably not going to endear her to the owners of the dog. Also, it would be considered trespassing and theft, she supposed. So instead, she squared her shoulders, took a couple of pictures documenting the dog's living conditions, and headed for the front door.

"I don't want any," snarled a testy voice from inside the house.

"I'm not selling anything," said Sam in as cheerful a voice as she could muster. She didn't feel like being cheerful at all. She felt very much like using a string of creatively assembled expletives. She quickly introduced herself instead.

"I don't want visitors, either," the neighbor elaborated.

"I won't be here long."

There was a pause from indoors. "I've said all I want to say about Arlo."

"Is Arlo your dog?" guessed Sam.

There was an irritated sigh from inside and an unshaved, large man wearing an undershirt and athletic shorts that were far too small for him answered the door. "What is it?"

"Well, for one, Arlo doesn't have any water. We all need water to survive," pointed out Sam, in case he didn't know. She was still biting her tongue from saying what she wanted to say. "If taking care of him is too much, I could help find local organizations or resources that could help. Maybe some dog training would help him fit in better with your family. Or a fence in the backyard to give him some extra space."

The man rolled his eyes as if he were being put upon in a completely unreasonable way. "I told my wife I didn't want the dog."

"Excuse me?"

"My wife," barked the man. "She divorced me and left. I told her to take Arlo with her, but she was going to live with a guy who was allergic. I told her I wasn't going to be able to take care of the dog."

"Wasn't able to? Or wouldn't?" asked Sam sweetly, a touch of steel right below the surface.

The man put his hands on his hips. "So you've come around here to badger me. Are you with the ASPCA or something?"

A smile quirked at Sam's lips. "As a matter of fact, I *am* with the ASPCA." She fished a card out of her purse. It was one of the many organizations Sam donated to and volunteered with.

She'd stuck the card in her wallet because that's where membership cards went, but she'd never thought twice about it. It was tucked in with memberships to the American Red Cross, World Wildlife Fund, The Nature Conservancy, and the March of Dimes.

The man glanced at the card quickly and backed up. "Look, I don't want any trouble."

"Neither do I," said Sam cheerfully. "Are we agreed that you don't want Arlo?"

"I don't."

"Would you be prepared to sign a statement to that effect?" asked Sam, still imagining the legal consequences if the man told the police she'd taken the dog. "And would it be all right with you if I were to re-home the dog?"

He tilted his head to one side. "Re-home where?"

"My house." Sam gave her address. "You could visit Arlo, if you like."

He gave a harsh laugh. "No, I don't need to visit Arlo."

"Right. Then I'll have you just sign the statement."

He scowled at her. "I don't have any paper."

Sam dove back into her bag, coming out with a small notebook and pen. "Here you are. Simply explain that you gifted Arlo to me, give a small description of Arlo, and sign and date it."

The man heaved a sigh. Then, with a grunt, he grabbed the notebook and pen, scrawled a statement, and thrust it back at Samantha.

"There. Now leave me in peace." He slammed the door behind him.

Samantha tapped at the door again.

He glared at her from inside.

"Vet records?" she asked loudly, so her voice would carry through the door.

"No vet records." The man walked away from the door.

Arlo gave her another plaintive wag of his tail as she walked over and stooped next to him. "Would you like to go home with me?" Sam asked in a gentle voice.

The little dog's tail thumped the ground, although he couldn't have known what she was saying. Sam quickly unchained him and took the collar from around his neck. Then she lifted his slight frame up and strode quickly back home as Arlo hesitantly licked her under her chin with his rough tongue.

When she walked in the house, Chad was relaxing on the sofa, watching some sort of sports program. He sat up straight, looking at Arlo. "What's *that*?"

"This is Arlo. We're rescuing him," said Sam. She carefully set down Arlo and went into the kitchen to find a suitable bowl to fill with water. Arlo regarded Chad anxiously.

"Rescuing him? Did you go to the shelter? I thought you were on your listening tour," said Chad slowly. "I can't keep up."

"No shelter. I rescued him from a neighbor who's had him chained up for ages. A very nasty neighbor." She watched as Arlo eagerly lapped up the water. "I need to call the vet."

"We have a vet?"

Sam walked over to get her notebook. The notebook had everything in it. It was basically a daily guide for Sam. She did everything it said to do because her past self had told her to do it.

"Making a list?" asked Chad. But it was barely a question. He'd lived with Sam long enough to know that's exactly what she'd be doing.

1. *Research vets*
2. *Make vet appointment*
3. *Purchase dog food, water bowl, dog bed, leash, and harness, flea medication, heartworm meds.*

She tapped her pencil against the paper as she thought. Arlo gave her a winsome grin.

"I'm going to take Arlo on a trip to the pet store. We're going to need some supplies."

Chad peered at the new member of the family. "He does look like an Arlo."

Sam considered this. "He looks much more like a Dash. But I wouldn't want to confuse the little guy. We'll stick with the name he came to us with."

"Want me to help you out at the store?" asked Chad. His eyes drifted back to the television as he asked, giving a distracted quality to his question.

"No, I think I'm good. It shouldn't take too long. I'll be back."

Arlo wasn't sure what he and Sam were doing next, but he appeared delighted to hop in the car to find out. Sam drove carefully to Sunset Ridge's scenic downtown to the pet store. She made a mental note to pick up a pet seatbelt for the car. And perhaps a tote bag that was designed for dogs to sit in. Arlo was definitely the right size for a tote bag.

The owner of the dog store gave Sam a polite smile when she came in and had kind words for Arlo, who was decidedly not looking his best. The owner became more animated and invested in Sam's visit when she started buying at least one item out of every category the store had. Shampoos, leashes, bowls, beds, toys, food, treats—the owner started collecting them at the check-out counter because Sam ran out of room in her cart. And the whole time, Arlo gave his engaging grin and wagged his little tail.

When Sam was finally done, the owner said cheerfully, "New fur baby? He looks like a love."

"Doesn't he? He's a rescue." A rescue from Sam's neighbor, that is. She paused, then briefly filled the woman in on the situation, hoping she could offer her some advice.

"Well, a trip to the vet for the poor little fella is definitely in order." The woman wrote down a couple of names of vet practices. "They can probably give you a salve for the chaffing around his neck. Arlo seems surprisingly well-socialized, so maybe the wife was able to handle that before she left her husband for the guy with the allergies. He may take some time to adjust to living inside, especially if you have a large home. His whole world was very limited for a long time."

Sam had taken out her phone and was taking notes. "Good points," she murmured as she typed. "So maybe not give him the run of the entire house at first."

"Baby steps. Then see how he does. He might adjust quickly." She reached out to rub Arlo, and he leaned his head into her hand. "He's a happy guy. I think you'll really enjoy him. Are you new to the area? I don't remember meeting you before."

Sam explained that she'd finished moving in days ago. "My husband and I, and now Arlo, are over in Maple Hills."

The shop owner said, "Oh goodness. Someone was telling me there was a mysterious death over there. George Turner, wasn't it?"

"I'm afraid so. Did you know George? I'd never met him."

The woman made a grimacing smile. "I did." She seemed to search for something nice to say about him. Then she quickly added, "He did a lot for the community. He was always lending a helping hand with committees, including downtown renewal." She paused. "He was a man with lots of ideas."

Sam nodded. "I've heard he could be difficult to get along with sometimes. Something of a powerful personality, maybe?"

Now the woman's smile turned rueful. "That's probably fair to say. But it takes a personality like that to get things done, I suppose."

The woman helped her load everything into the car. Then she gave Arlo a few treats for the road and waved as they drove away.

Chad helped Samantha on the other end, saying nothing about the fact that their new home was turning into a dog wonderland. "Looks like you got some good stuff," he said.

"Once I got in there, I realized how much we needed to get," said Sam. "The owner was very helpful, though." She filled in Chad on the suggestions the owner had made.

"Got it. We'll give that a go and see how he does." Chad watched as Sam carefully took the packaging off the different items and started setting the dog items out. "I know I only ran to the store yesterday, but I totally didn't remember the other things I needed there because I was focused on the picnic food. Is there anything you need while I'm there?"

"Hmm? No, I have to make a real list when I do my Sunday night meal planning. I'll be at the store tomorrow to get the ingredients."

Chad grinned at her. "Oh, right. I always forget about Sunday night meal planning."

"It makes life easier, I swear. You can't wait until then to pick up your items? I could get them tomorrow."

"It's okay. I probably need an excuse to get out of the house, anyway. I'll be back soon."

Chad left and Sam continued setting out bowls, beds, toys, and other things. She wasn't sure when Arlo had last eaten, so she fed the dog. He consumed it ravenously, making Sam press her lips together. She wondered if he'd been as regularly fed as his portly owner had been.

The doorbell rang, making Arlo lift his head curiously before continuing to eat. There was no explosion of barking, which made sense, considering he was accustomed to being outside all the time.

Sam opened the door to see the woman who'd shrunk back from her conversation with George Turner at the picnic. Sam hadn't gotten that far on her listening tour after discovering Arlo. The woman had her auburn hair tied back in a ponytail, was holding a container, and was wearing an uncertain smile. "Hi," she said. "I'm Olivia Stanton."

"Nice to meet you," said Sam with a big smile. "Won't you come inside?" She reminded herself she shouldn't pepper the woman with questions.

"Oh, I hate to intrude," Olivia said, looking even more uncertain. "You must still be working on moving in."

"All done with that," said Sam. She gestured for Olivia to come in and Olivia, after a moment of hesitation, did just that.

"I wanted to bring you a meal to welcome you to the neighborhood," she said. She gave a small smile. "My husband was appalled that I hadn't been over yet. It's been a little hectic lately." Olivia gave a forced laugh, but looked to be on the verge of tears.

That sounded like a strike against Olivia's husband, whoever he was.

"You shouldn't worry about that. Here, come sit down. I appreciate the meal. It looks wonderful."

Olivia brightened a little at the compliment. "Chicken Tetrazzini. I hope you'll enjoy it."

"I'm sure we will," said Sam kindly.

Maybe it was the tone of kindness that was the final straw. Olivia burst into the tears that had been threatening to fall. "I'm so sorry," she gasped through the violence of the emotion.

Sam grabbed a nearby box of tissues and thrust them at Olivia. "You're fine," she said soothingly, letting Olivia cry it out. She poured a glass of ice water for her and set it on the table beside Olivia. Arlo, finally finished with his meal, trotted in to look worriedly at Olivia.

It was Arlo who was able to stop Olivia's tears. She hiccupped for a few seconds, staring at the little dog. "Is that . . . ?"

"Arlo? Yes, it is."

Arlo leaned against Sam's legs and she gently picked him up. He nestled back against Sam and gave Olivia a little canine grin.

"Oh, my gosh. I'm *so* glad you've got that poor guy. I'd thought a million times about taking him off that chain, but Dominic isn't a fan of animals."

That was strike two against Olivia's husband in Sam's book. She said, "Well, the owner grudgingly gave him to me this afternoon. We're still getting acquainted."

"It looks like he's already settling in," said Olivia. She wiped a few tears away, then delicately blew her nose into a tissue. Arlo trotted over to her and bumped his small head against her leg. "What a sweetie," she said softly, reaching down to rub him.

"Are you okay?" asked Sam. "I know we don't really know each other, but I do care about the answer to that question. Can I help you out?"

This made Olivia's tears start up again, although this time they slowed to a trickle. "Oh, I'm not sure that anybody can help me, Sam. But you're very sweet to offer."

Sam said slowly, "I know this is none of my business. But I saw you at the picnic, briefly, with George." As the color drained from Olivia's face, Sam added, "I don't think George must have been a very nice man. He was looking very sly when he spoke to you. And I thought at the time that you looked upset. That you wanted to get away from him."

Olivia was silent for a few moments. Then she looked over at Sam as if trying to weigh whether or not she could trust her. She must have seen something that made her want to try because she spoke in a halting voice. "It's a secret. Something I need to keep from my husband. He'll divorce me and leave me with nothing if he knows."

"An affair?" Sam asked.

Olivia nodded.

"With George Turner?"

Olivia nodded again. Arlo gave her a beseeching look, and she gently scooped him up and put him on her lap. She rubbed him absentmindedly. "Such a mistake. The affair with George, I mean. I don't know what I was thinking. I should never have given that man any power over me. I knew better. But at first, he was different. So attentive and flattering. I hadn't gotten that kind of attention and praise from a man in years."

Sam decided that was a third strike against Dominic. "I'm sure that must have been irresistible."

Olivia looked relieved that Sam seemed to understand. "Yes, it was. He and I crossed paths during various Maple Hills events. We both volunteered around Sunset Ridge, too. I was feeling just so . . . trapped. Trapped in my life, trapped in my unhappy marriage. George seemed to be the answer to all my problems." She gave a short laugh. "I must have been out of my mind."

"You mentioned that you gave him power over you," said Sam.

"Yes. What I didn't realize about George was that he was as much of a control freak as Dom is. I put myself right where he wanted me—in a position where I was beholden to him to keep quiet."

Sam raised her eyebrows. "George was going to expose your affair?"

Olivia shrugged. "He had nothing to lose. He was single. And he knew I depend on Dominic for everything. Money, social status—everything."

Sam shook her head. "I don't understand why George would tell Dominic about the affair."

"Just because he wanted to watch me squirm. He wasn't being discreet anymore. I was up all night, worried that the entire neighborhood was going to find out. I couldn't stand everyone staring at me or talking about me behind my back. And, of course, if Dominic found out, it would be terrible."

"Maybe you should consider leaving Dominic," said Sam in a serious voice.

A panicked look crossed Olivia's features. "I can't do that. I'd have to start all over again. Move in with my parents. It's not an option."

"Okay," said Sam calmly. "Got it."

Olivia looked down at her hands, which were folded in her lap. "It was so upsetting how George was so determined to seek me out at the picnic. I was trying to avoid having to talk to him. I think he was enjoying tormenting me. He wanted to upset me, to make me feel uncomfortable. I was sure Dom was going to notice."

Sam said carefully, "Olivia, if you're afraid of Dominic, there are resources I can connect you with. If he's harming you in any way."

Olivia relaxed a bit, stroking Arlo. "No, Dom wouldn't hurt a fly. Not physically nor emotionally. But he'd divorce me in a skinny second. He's very image conscious." She gave another short laugh. "I must be, too. Because my main worry is losing money and my standing in the community."

"So nobody knows about any of this."

"Just you and me, now that George is gone," said Olivia.

"So you haven't had any uncomfortable questions from the police, I'm guessing."

"Well, they spoke to me at the picnic, of course, just like they did everyone else. But nothing pointed—only general questions about George, his allergy, and who'd been speaking with him." Olivia gave her a horrified look. "You won't tell the cops about our affair, will you?"

Sam shook her head. "No. Although it might be better if you did. Even though you're sure no one else knows about it, it would be worse if the police find out about it than if you volunteer the information."

Arlo leaned against Olivia's chest, regarding Sam solemnly.

Oliva said fervently, "I'm not volunteering anything. It was a terrible mistake and has nothing to do with George's death. I'll send them on a wild goose chase if I inform the cops about our affair. No way."

"Have you had any thoughts about who might have wanted to murder George? Does anyone come to mind?"

Olivia snorted. "*Everyone* comes to mind. No one liked George. But I know he was having problems with one particular person. His son, Marcus."

Sam remembered hearing from Nora that Marcus and George didn't have the best relationship.

Olivia continued, "I didn't tell you how George's and my affair ended. George was the one who called it off. He'd found a younger woman to date. He rubbed that in my face," she added bitterly. "I thought *I* was the younger woman."

"Well, you were," Sam said. "You mean he started seeing someone even younger?"

"That's right. She worked retail and seemed to be some sort of hanger-on. I guess she must have had to work yesterday, or she'd have been at the picnic. Anyway, Marcus was very upset by his dad dating this young woman. The only reason I know about it is because Marcus was letting his dad have it in the grocery store when I was in there one day. He said his father was making a fool of himself."

Sam said, "That seems like a very public place for a personal argument."

Olivia shrugged. "Maybe it's because George wouldn't take his phone calls. George had told me when we were together that he usually avoided Marcus's calls because he was always asking for money. He sometimes didn't answer the door when he was there, too."

"Could you hear what Marcus was telling his dad when you were in the grocery store?"

"Sure," said Olivia. "The whole store could probably hear it. Marcus thought the girl wasn't educated and didn't have any class. He thought she was a gold-digger. Maybe he thought George was going to marry her and change his will so that Marcus wasn't the beneficiary anymore, who knows?" She sighed. "This whole thing is such a mess. I should never have had an affair with George. You know, I still care for Dom. I was so crazy about him when we met in college."

"You've been married for a while then," said Sam lightly.

Olivia nodded. "It feels like a lifetime. He was always really ambitious. I guess I found that appealing, since it's not a trait I have. As time went on, though, he's gotten so much more serious. We've gotten off-track somehow, and I think it's up to me to get things back *on*-track." She stood up, putting Arlo carefully on the floor and looking a little shy. "You must be easy to talk to. I'm sorry I've been bending your ear like this. I just came by to give you the food."

"Maybe you needed someone to talk it over with. It's hard keeping things pent-up like that. You can bend my ear anytime." Sam stood, too. "While you're here, is there anything you want changed in Maple Hills? I'm planning on running for the open HOA president spot."

"Really?" Oliva looked surprised. "Wow, you've just moved here."

"I know you said Dominic was ambitious—is he running for the spot, too?"

Olivia said, "Dom? No. That's too small potatoes for him. I can't think of anything off the top of my head that I'd like to see changed in the neighborhood, though. If I think of something, I'll let you know."

"Thanks for that. I was also looking at volunteering in the community now that Chad and I have settled in. Is there an organization that you recommend?"

Olivia flushed. "That's been something that's on my list to do for such a long time."

"Well, life can get busy, can't it? You work remotely, I'm guessing?"

The flush deepened. "No, I decided not to. Dom is doing so well, and I didn't see a point in contributing to that. Do you work?"

"Not anymore," said Sam, not particularly wanting to go into the details of the app again. "But I get restless if I spend too much time at the house. You must spend a lot of time cleaning and doing yardwork."

Now Olivia looked guilty. "No, we hire out for those things."

Sam was at a total loss at that point. She knew she'd go out of her mind if she were at home all day with no work, no volunteering, and no tasks around the house. No wonder Olivia had an affair. She was probably simply trying to fill the hours in her day.

Olivia seemed to want to redeem herself in Sam's eyes. "We could volunteer together," she said brightly. "How about if we research the different options, decide on one, and put it on our schedule?"

"That sounds like a plan," said Sam with a smile.

Olivia appeared relieved. "Perfect. I'll take a look at it and get back to you. Well, it was so good to talk to you, Sam."

"Thanks for dinner. I really appreciate it."

Chapter Six

After Olivia left, Sam sat down with her notebook. She added Olivia to her list of suspects, which included Nora, Julia, and Marcus. She'd created something of a suspect scorecard, rating various suspects on their likelihood of having murdered George. Right now, Julia was fairly high on her list, but only because she hadn't yet spoken with Marcus, George's son and heir. She studied her scorecard and mulled over the feasibility of having a murder incident room with a whiteboard and photos of the victim and suspects.

Her musings were interrupted as Chad returned with groceries. "Can I give you a hand bringing them in?" called Sam.

"No need. It's just a couple of things." He started unpacking two small bags and putting the groceries away. "How are things going here?"

"Oh, they're fine. Olivia Stanton came by with dinner for us."

Chad joined her in the sunroom. "Did she? That was nice." He thought for a moment. "Let's see. Stanton. That name's familiar."

"You might have met her husband at the picnic. His name is Dominic, although I think people might call him Dom."

Chad snapped his fingers. "That's right. He's a bigwig in finance, I think."

"In finance? Here in Sunset Ridge?" Sam thought of the tiny bank branches in the town.

"He works remotely for one of the big banks in Charlotte, I think. Seemed like a great guy," he said cheerfully.

Sam was starting to think that Chad believed *everyone* to be a great guy. Perhaps he wasn't the most perceptive of men.

Chad looked at her a little more closely. "You look like you're keyed up. Didn't you have a good visit with Olivia?"

Maybe he was more perceptive than she gave him credit for. "It was nice," she said. She didn't feel like exposing Olivia's secret. Chad was a sociable person with a bad habit of not keeping secrets. Those two traits didn't go together very well. "I'm just restless, as usual."

Chad surveyed Arlo, who was occupying Sam's lap again. "He seems a little nervous of me, doesn't he?"

Sam glanced down at Arlo. His small body seemed very tense and his ears were pulled back slightly. He averted his gaze from Chad.

"Well, it's probably going to take time. After all, he was living with a man who was treating him horribly. The poor dog is probably scarred. Maybe you can try giving him some treats in a little while."

"That's a good idea," said Chad. "What are you planning on doing now? Want to watch that movie?"

A movie was the last thing Sam wanted to do right then, as her brain was whirling with different thoughts. She needed something calming. "I don't think I'd be able to sit still. I think I'll work on my Christmas cards."

"Sam. It's September," groaned Chad.

Samantha grinned at him. "Well, my mother always said idle hands are the devil's instruments. Anyway, doing something a little mindless is relaxing for me."

"Don't they have wine for that?" asked Chad in a teasing voice.

"It's not five o'clock yet," said Sam. "And I've already violated my rule yesterday because a neighbor wanted me to have a drink with them."

Chad definitely knew better than to make Sam break the various rules she had for herself. "Got it. How did your listening tour go earlier? You didn't tell me what conclusions you came to. What does everyone want for Maple Hills?"

"Oh, the typical things. Safety, programming, streetlights, speed bumps, a playground upgrade—stuff like that. They all did say I had their votes."

Chad said, "Of course they did. They'd be insane not to." He walked over and gave Sam a kiss on her forehead as Arlo shrank back. Chad frowned.

"It'll take time," repeated Sam. She gently picked up Arlo and sat him down on the floor. Then she went to her desk, where she found the container of Christmas cards she'd ordered earlier in the year. She also pulled out a stack of papers held together by a binder clip.

"Oh my gosh," said Chad. "Is that the Christmas card list?"

"Are you surprised? We know a lot of people."

Chad said, "I didn't think we knew *that* many people. Are you sure the list doesn't need to be updated? That some folks shouldn't be crossed off? Some of them might have died in the interval. I can think of several likely candidates."

"I haven't heard of any updates that need to be made. Once you're on my Christmas card list, you're on there. You don't come off unless I'm presented with a death certificate."

Chad gave her an anxious look, then smiled in relief. "You're joking. Good. I was getting worried."

"Well, sort of joking. I do take my list pretty seriously. Plus, I'm adding new neighbors now that I have the HOA directory. I'd like to write a small personal note on each card."

"Weren't you saying that one of our neighbors is likely a murderer? Shouldn't we reserve the right to strike someone from the list if they end up going to prison?"

Sam pretended to consider this seriously, tilting her head to one side. "Hmm. That's a good question. I'll have to see what the policies are for mail at the prison before answering that." She grinned at him.

But Chad didn't seem to be paying attention. "I'm still not convinced George's death wasn't just an awful accident. The cops are probably trying to scare up something to do."

Sam said, "The more I hear about George, the less I think it was an accident. In fact, I really can't see how it could be an accident at all. George was apparently quite painstaking about avoiding other people's food. He brought his own meals to every gathering. No, somebody wanted to get rid of him. I've already run across quite a few contenders."

"Like who?" asked Chad.

Since she'd already put all her suspects and their motives on her list and murder suspect scorecard, she didn't especially feel like covering them in-depth with Chad. A brief overview seemed appropriate. "Well, there's George's son. He apparently was having a rough spell with his father over money."

"Who? That surgeon I met?" asked Chad with surprise. "Was George asking his son for money?"

"No, it was apparently the other way around."

Chad frowned. "A US surgeon with no money? That's what the older woman at the picnic was telling us. Nora. I still find it really hard to believe."

"Maybe he had a ton of school debt. Or maybe he's a gambler or a drug addict. Who knows? That's just something I've heard. Of course, we have to take it with a grain of salt."

"I'd say," said Chad. "Why would he even be at the picnic in the first place if he wasn't getting along with his dad?"

"From what I understand, Marcus was having a tough time getting in touch with his father. George wasn't answering his phone calls or even answering the door when Marcus showed up. Maybe Marcus thought it was a good opportunity to catch him somewhere. Somewhere where George couldn't ignore him. Then there's Nora."

"Our nosy neighbor?" asked Chad, sounding surprised.

"I'll agree she seems like an unlikely suspect, because of her age. But the application of an allergen to a salad makes for an easy murder method, even for seniors. She seemed rather delighted at George's demise. He'd caused a lot of trouble for her with the HOA."

"Got it." He paused. "You're taking this seriously, aren't you?"

"I take everything seriously, don't I? Solving this case almost seems like a brainteaser."

Chad said, "I wouldn't have thought you needed anything to occupy your brain with right now, but you always manage to surprise and delight me, Sam. Anyone else on your suspect list?"

"Julia Harper. She had a long-standing feud with George after she worked with him on a local park project. Apparently, the trouble ended up extending to Maple Hills." Sam stopped at that point, not wanting to expose Olivia's secret. But Olivia Stanton was definitely on her suspect list, too.

Chad gave a low whistle. "That's a lot to unpack. No wonder you're delving into Christmas cards."

"It's important to stay busy, don't you think?"

Chad clearly did *not* think so. He was an expert at doing very little and enjoying every moment. Sam was sometimes envious of his ability to relax. He reached out tentatively to Arlo again, who was curled up on Sam. Arlo pulled back farther into Sam's embrace.

"Give it time," suggested Sam.

The next morning, Sam woke up early to Arlo gently licking her face. She chuckled and cuddled him for a few quiet minutes before getting up to get ready for her day. Sam called the vet's office bright and early. In a small town, she had the feeling it might be hard to get a new patient appointment, especially one as immediate as Sam wanted it to happen. But she was in luck.

"Actually, we have a cancelation at ten. Would you be able to make that?"

Sam could. Even better, the vet had new patient paperwork on their website for Sam to download, fill out, and take with her.

While filling out the paperwork, Sam leaped into her usual multitasking. She called Mandy and Alfred's doctor's office, although they'd advised her they'd likely direct her over to the collections office.

She held on the line as she completed Arlo's paperwork. Then she put the phone in her pocket and started putting together supper in the slow cooker. She finished preparing it and was still on hold.

Then she cleaned three bathrooms, two of which didn't need any cleaning at all. Still on hold.

At the one-hour-fifteen-minute mark, the call dropped, something they'd also warned Sam that they'd encountered.

Sam pursed her lips. Unacceptable.

This motivated her to call the collections agency. A determinedly cheerful woman answered the phone. Sam identified herself as Mandy, then launched into an explanation of a canceled check, a software migration at her healthcare provider, and problems reaching anyone who could help. Sam had, naturally, created a script before the phone call.

Before she could finish her script, however, the pleasant-sounding woman told her she'd have to speak with the healthcare provider.

"But they're telling me I have to talk with you because the bill is in collections," pointed out Sam in a reasonable voice.

"Sorry, I can't really help you on my end with payments that weren't credited. I don't have access to their computer systems. You'll need to speak to a customer service rep over at the doctor's office for that." And the woman politely but firmly got off the phone.

It was the type of situation that made Sam grit her teeth. However, the dentist assured her that gritting her teeth was an unhealthy habit, so she decided to double-down on fixing Mandy and Alfred's problem instead.

Sam set about gathering a bunch of things that she needed to do. Her Christmas cards, naturally. Her notebook, where she might as well do the meal planning for the *following* week, although the current week had just started. She even dug up some knitting from a long ago, abandoned project. She loaded everything into a laptop bag along with her computer, some granola bars, and a water bottle. Then she threw the bag into the car.

It was time then for Arlo's appointment. The little guy was pathetically happy about another trip in the car, although Sam was sad this car ride wouldn't end up at the pet store but at the vet. She hoped they'd be good with him and that Arlo wouldn't end up scared of the place.

Sam, as usual, had high expectations. She started relaxing when they walked in and the receptionist came out from around the desk to love on Arlo. She relaxed a bit more when treats were offered to the delighted dog. Things continued in this vein with a very brief waiting room wait, an empathetic and professional veterinarian, and lots of treats while Arlo was examined and received immunizations.

"I think you've got a great little guy," said the vet. Arlo beamed at her.

With that errand completed to her total satisfaction, Sam realized the next one likely would give her some trouble. She got

Arlo back home, saw him settle happily in a sunbeam in his new dog bed, and headed back out the door again. It was time to take on Mandy and Albert's doctor's office, at the hospital branch.

Sam squared her shoulders as she walked in. She politely explained she needed to talk to someone in billing as soon as possible. The front desk seemed rather surprised at this. "You should call."

Sam bared her teeth in a smile. "Sadly, the billing department has made that completely impossible, perhaps by design. Since this matter needs immediate resolution, I'll plan on speaking with a billing manager in person."

The woman at the front desk gave her a doubtful look. "That could take some time."

"Fortunately, I came prepared with plenty of provisions." Sam settled into a corner chair where she could see the entire room. Then she plugged in her laptop, pulled out her planner and lists, her Christmas cards, and a pen. She left the knitting in for the time being, mostly because she could no longer remember what she was knitting in the first place and the item itself offered her no hints.

She delved into various tasks while there was murmured, worried chatting among the receptionists. Then there was an equally concerned phone call, presumably to the billing department. Sam had completed only four Christmas cards when someone hurried out to the lobby to join her.

Sam gave the man her most brilliant smile. Then she gave him a practiced recap of the phone calls, the disconnected calls, the software migration, the merger, the collections issues, the mixed messages, and the emotional distress. Then she presented her fait accompli, the proof of payment.

The man looked stunned. Sam was sure to back up her statements with the paperwork Mandy and Alfred had given her, which she'd carefully enclosed in sheet protectors, labeled with sticky notes, and contained in a large binder. He slowly flipped through the pages in the binder.

"I don't see any reason this issue should cost me any more time," stated Sam solemnly.

The man didn't seem to be able to voice any reason why it should, either.

Sam continued, "What I need from you is a receipt of payment, a screenshot of our account indicating the payment issue is resolved, and an email to the collections agency, terminating their efforts to collect the money. I need to be copied on that email."

The man continued nodding. "And an apology," he said, although his uncomfortable manner hinted he wasn't particularly good at them.

"No apology needed," said Sam cheerfully. "A resolution to the matter is the only thing needed. And, by resolution, I hope you understand I won't be able to leave this office until I have the receipt and screenshot in hand, and the email to the collections agency in my inbox."

The man scurried away to handle it all while Sam put away the binder and continued working on the other things she'd brought with her to while away the time.

Ten minutes later, it was all finished to Sam's satisfaction. "Pleasure doing business with you," said Sam politely, extending her hand.

The man quickly shook it, likely hoping Sam would disappear as quickly as she'd appeared.

As Sam drove home, she reflected on how nice it was to be starting her day with a win. Actually, it was more than a single win. Arlo had a successful vet visit and had checked out far healthier than Sam had feared he might. This was followed by resolving Mandy and Alfred's billing issue. Buoyed by these achievements, Sam felt as though she might want to take on the world. Or, at least, another project for the day.

She found an opportunity when she was pulling into the neighborhood. She saw a man in his mid-30s removing boxes from George Turner's house and loading them into an expensive SUV. Nora was looking out her window at the proceedings. Sam decided she definitely didn't want a conversation with Nora right now, but she did want to speak with the man she guessed was probably Marcus, George's semi-estranged son.

Sam pulled her car into the driveway and hopped out. The man watched as she walked up. "I'm Samantha Prescott. I was at the picnic Saturday, and I wanted to tell you how very sorry I am about your father's death."

The man relaxed a little, although his green eyes still regarded her warily. "Marcus Turner," he said automatically. "And thank you. It's been a real shock."

Sam said, "Can I give you a hand here? At least, it looks as if you might be clearing out your dad's house. I'm fairly good at organizing." Sam actually considered herself exceptional at organizing, but was determined to be modest.

Marcus opened his mouth as if to turn her down, but paused, his eyes taking in Sam's tall, slender frame and thick, dark-brown hair. "That seems like quite an imposition," he hedged.

"Oh, it would be my pleasure to help," said Sam. "Do you have different piles, I'm guessing? One for trash, one for charity, and one for things you'd like to keep?"

Marcus gave her a boyish grin. "Actually, there are only two piles. I've decided there's nothing of my father's that I'd really to like to keep."

"Gotcha. Well, that makes things easier. I can make a trip to Goodwill, if you've got a load to take. Or I can help you identify trash and charity items."

Marcus said, "If you'd like to step inside, I can show you what I've been doing."

Sam saw the curtains flutter next door and had the feeling Nora was taking notes as she and Marcus stepped into George's house.

Chapter Seven

George's house was older, but in excellent condition. Even though Marcus had been going through everything and setting items in piles, she could tell it was kept spotless when George was alive. The wood floors gleamed, the granite surfaces in the kitchen were immaculate. Even the stainless-steel refrigerator was remarkably fingerprint-free. It seemed as if George, in life, had been a very careful housekeeper.

Marcus must have read her mind. "Dad was something of a neat freak," he said wryly. "The house has never been messier than it is right now, with me tearing through it to clear it." He paused. "You know, I'm actually feeling like I need a break from all this. I appreciate your offer, but I'm not going to put you to work after all. Your appearance reminded me I've been clearing things out for the last few hours. Want to have a seat? At least I haven't gotten as far as the furniture yet, so there are places to sit down."

"Are you planning to have an estate sale?" asked Sam as she sank into a toile chair.

"Garage sale, more like," said Marcus, perching on an antique settee.

Sam glanced around the room. "That might be the easiest, but these are nice things. Lots of well-preserved antiques."

Marcus nodded. "Yeah. I've thought about finding someone to help me run an estate sale. But I think it's one of those things that might end up being more trouble than it's worth. Right now, I'm feeling like clearing everything out is healing for me."

"Right. Grief is tough to manage. I'd imagine that going through your dad's things could help you."

Marcus gave her a rueful look. "It's not so much grief. Maybe it's more of a mixture of things. Anger, frustration with Dad, and probably guilt, too. I could have been a better son. Dad could have been a better father."

"Family relationships are the worst," said Sam.

"It sounds like you speak from experience."

Sam nodded. As usual, she declined to speak about her own family. Her parents had proven to be lazy, poor at raising children, and greedy after she'd sold her app.

Marcus seemed to realize that Sam wasn't going to elaborate. He said, "Well, sounds like we've been in the same boat. Like I said, I've had a weird mix of feelings. I do feel guilty about not being a better kid. I also feel guilty about not saving him on Saturday."

"I don't think there was anything you could do, Marcus."

He said, "I could have carried an EpiPen with me. I knew how allergic Dad was. I also knew he wasn't great about carrying one himself. I think he'd gotten complacent, having dealt with the allergy all his life."

"My understanding is that he'd brought his own food to the picnic."

Marcus nodded. "He did. That was his usual practice. That way, he felt like no one else had to worry about *his* allergy." He gave a rueful smile. "Dad wasn't the most thoughtful person, but he was good at managing his almond allergy."

"So someone must have tampered with his plate. He certainly didn't put almonds on his food."

Marcus gave a small grin. "Nope. Dad definitely wasn't interested in poisoning himself. Although it means that most of the neighborhood is now a suspect. Present company excluded, of course."

"You really shouldn't exclude anyone. Although it wouldn't make much sense for either my husband or myself to tamper with your father's food. We just moved into Maple Hills this week and hadn't even met your dad before the picnic."

Marcus looked a bit deflated at her mention of a husband. "Ah. Well, I think we can safely strike you both off the list. Naturally, the police currently think I'm an excellent candidate."

"I'm sure that's all routine. Family members are usually suspects." Sam paused. "I'm a little surprised you were at the picnic at all. You don't live in Maple Hills, do you?"

"No, I live in another subdivision across town. The only reason I attended the picnic is because Dad wanted me there. He liked to show off his family," said Marcus dryly.

"That must mean you're someone who's good to show off," said Sam in a perky tone.

"I'll admit to being a surgeon," said Marcus. "It's why my dad was even slightly proud of me. He hadn't been speaking with me recently—he was avoiding my phone calls. I was happy to show up and see him. I couldn't believe what happened to him."

Sam gave him a perfunctory smile. But she was thinking about the moment that George had collapsed at the picnic. How she'd jumped into action, commanding neighbors to call 911. How a young mother who'd just taken CPR classes had tried to revive George. Why hadn't Marcus, a surgeon, and someone who most certainly would have a lot more medical training and background than the mom, jumped in to help save his father?

Marcus seemed to read her mind. "Thanks to you for all your help with my dad when he was dying. I'm mortified that I was frozen in place. In the hospital, it's totally different. I view everyone through a lens, in a way. I've got distance, some perspective. But when Dad fell to the ground, I couldn't even seem to move. Like I say, I feel guilty I couldn't save him."

"I don't think anyone could save him at that point, not without an EpiPen. You shouldn't feel guilty. Of course, it was different, having your parent in such a state."

Marcus gave a short laugh. "If only the police agreed with you. I think they find my inaction another sign that I wanted my father out of the way. But my father and I ordinarily got along very well with each other, aside from the last few weeks. I respected him and all he'd accomplished in his life. He'd had nothing growing up, and his parents hadn't been very supportive of him. He was a self-made man."

Sam could hear the pride in his voice as he spoke about his father. "Was your dad supportive of you, growing up? Did he break the cycle?"

"He was very supportive. And he always cheered me on when the going got rough at school. There are a ton of really challenging classes, starting in high school and going all the way through the medical degree. He always encouraged me to do better and told me I could do it." He shrugged. "And I did."

"Was it just you and your dad, then?" asked Sam.

"Well, it has been since I was seven or eight. Mom just up and left one day." He gave another shrug, but there was a flash of pain in his eyes. "We didn't hear from her after that. So Dad also had to take on being a single parent in the middle of it all. Fortunately, he was well-off enough, even back then, to hire some help for some of the cooking and cleaning."

Sam said, "Did you tell the cops all this? Your background with your father?"

Marcus gave a short laugh. "I sketched it out a little, but I don't think it made much of a difference. They were more interested in the here and now—what I knew about Dad's will and that kind of thing."

"His will?" asked Sam innocently.

"Right. I guess the cops thought I'd murdered my father to inherit his money. But I don't know anything about the will. Dad was always someone who kept stuff like that close to his chest. He wasn't exactly going to open up to me to show me his will or go over his financial situation."

Sam said, "Have you come across it while you've been cleaning up?"

He gave her a smile, but it didn't reach his eyes. "No. And I haven't been looking for it. Although, I've been careful to make sure I'm not throwing away any important documents as I'm trashing stuff. I'm sure the police have probably already gotten in touch with Dad's lawyer, so they probably know more than I do. I'm guessing the lawyer has a copy and there's probably one filed here somewhere. Maybe another at the courthouse. But the will wasn't the only thing the police were focused on."

Sam said, "I'm guessing they were probably asking you who was standing near your father. They asked me the same thing."

"Right. They wanted to know who was near his food. The problem was that *everyone* was near his food. Plus, Dad was a grazer. He wasn't going to start eating his food and gulp it straight down. Someone would come up to speak with him, and he'd set his plate down on the picnic table so he could speak with his hands."

After Marcus mentioned this, Sam could remember George waving his hands around as he gesticulated about various things. It made sense that he wouldn't be guarding his food. It made sense that he wouldn't guard his food to begin with, considering that he'd have thought he was in the presence of his neighbors and, perhaps, friends.

"Was there anyone in particular that your father experienced trouble with in the neighborhood? Did he ever talk about anybody in terms of problems he was having with them?" asked Sam.

"Sure, he talked about everybody. His next-door neighbor drove him nuts. I can't remember her name, but she's the nosiest person I've ever met. And she wasn't crazy about Dad, either."

"Nora?" asked Sam.

"That's it. Nora. Then there's Julia Harper, too. I don't know if you've met her yet."

Sam nodded. "I have, actually. She and your dad weren't getting along?"

"That's an understatement. And it's been going on forever. Julia and Dad were working on a community park project and they were at each other's throats the whole time. Dad said Julia was trying to control the whole project, but since he was the project coordinator, he was standing in her way. That wasn't her role; she was only supposed to be the project designer. Dad said she wanted full creative control and saw Dad as an obstacle to realizing her vision for the park."

Sam said, "I'm sure it was worse with them being neighbors, too. That would make things really awkward."

"True. Anyway, I've only got Dad's side of the story, but he said she was being completely unreasonable. She also blamed him for taking credit for parts of the project she thought she'd been responsible for. On top of that, she seemed to hold a personal grudge against Dad's decisions regarding the distribution of the project budget."

Sam said, "It sounds like Julia was taking things personally."

"Oh, it was definitely personal. From the way Dad was talking, the park project became a symbol of her struggle against him within the HOA board. Julia was trying to do some sort of home improvement project and flipped out when he didn't approve it. Dad also said he thought she was a heavy drinker, which was making her more emotionally unstable."

Sam remembered Julia tossing back alcohol during her visit. She'd thought at the time it might be a reaction to George's sudden death. Now it sounded like it could be the sign of a problem instead.

"Was there anyone else besides Nora and Julia?" asked Sam.

Marcus smiled at her, but there was a slight edge to his voice as he said, "Now you're sounding more like the cops. Who hated your dad? Who was standing next to him? I wasn't paying that much attention. Frankly, I was just pleased that Dad had asked me to be there. I was trying to act like the perfect son, so he'd be proud of me. The last thing on my mind was murdering my father or watching to see if someone slipped almonds into his food. All I could tell the police was there was one person who definitely *wasn't* involved in Dad's death. That odd woman who never really joined in."

"Pris," said Sam. Pris was on her listening tour, of course, although she was thinking she needed to be bumped up. Perhaps Pris needed some sort of help.

"Right. Whatever. At any rate, she was yards away from Dad at every second of the picnic." He shook his head. "I get being shy, but if you're wanting to blend into a group, it's easier if you don't stand out so much."

"Is that why she was standing back? Because she's shy?"

Marcus said, "I'm hazarding a guess. Maybe she's agoraphobic. Or dealing with trauma of some kind." He sighed. "Sorry, I'm usually a lot more compassionate when talking about other people. I'd say she definitely has an issue that a healthcare professional should help her address."

Sam nodded. "I thought much the same at the picnic. I'd noticed her, too, right there on the fringes of the group, holding back."

"Maybe it's a case of social anxiety," said Marcus. "At any rate, she was nowhere near Dad at any time."

Sam glanced around the house. Although all of George's belongings were being dismantled, it was being done in an organized, thoughtful manner. Maybe the apple didn't fall far from the tree when it came to Marcus. She stood, smiling at him. "I've held you up too long. It was good to meet you."

He stood too, giving her a rueful grin. "Sure you can't help me stall any longer?"

"You had the right idea at the beginning—knock it all out as quickly as possible. I'm sorry again about your father. Good luck with the cleaning."

Chapter Eight

Sam got back into her car and headed the short distance to her house. Marcus had seemed like a genuine person. She didn't get the sense of any artifice when he spoke about his dad or their relationship. But still, it felt as if he'd chosen to hold some things back. That was natural, of course, but it made her wonder more about his financial issues and the fact he expressed little interest in the will.

When she walked inside the house, Arlo came running to greet her, tail wagging. Sam picked him up and Arlo snuggled against her. His fur was soft, although his coat was mismatched. Maybe he could pick up on her distracted mood because he gave her a comforting nuzzle under her chin.

"Want to help me in the kitchen?" she asked Arlo.

Arlo wagged his tail again, indicating he'd like to help as much as possible.

Sam set him gently on the bay window seat and consulted her planner for the evening's meal. She hoped her past self had made life easy for her future self by choosing something simple to put together. To her relief, she saw it was meatballs and rice in the crock-pot. She pulled out the meatballs, cream of mushroom soup, onion soup mix, and beef bouillon, and put them in the slow cooker with a bit of water. Then she double-checked to make sure she had the sour cream that she'd add toward the end of the cooking cycle. Arlo watched her with interest from his perch on the seat, head cocked to one side. Then he settled down with a chew toy, happily dividing his time between chewing and looking with interest at gray squirrels prancing around outside the window.

"Well, that was easy," said Sam absently as she finished preparing the meal. She glanced around the kitchen to see if there was any mess to clean up, but she'd cleaned up as she'd gone along. She wiped down the counters with a paper towel, just in case. Then she looked at her watch. Mandy and Alfred wouldn't be home from work yet. She'd run by there and hand over their paperwork when it was after five.

Chad strolled into the kitchen, sniffing. "Hey, everything smells good in here."

Arlo put his head down on his paws, looking suspiciously at Chad.

Sam snorted. "You're being nice. I just turned on the slow cooker, so we won't be able to smell anything good for at least an hour."

"Maybe I'm simply *expecting* being able to smell something good," said Chad with a grin. "How is everything going? Have you fixed the universe today? It would be all in a day's work for you."

"Don't be silly," said Sam. "That's far too big a task. You know how I dislike setting myself up for failure. Knocking out small things a bit at a time is a lot better. But yes, I had a successful day. Arlo is a healthy little guy, for one thing."

Arlo gave Chad a wary look, as if warning him not to approach.

"That's good," said Chad. "No parasites or whatnot?"

"Well, they have to get the results back from the lab on that stuff and the bloodwork. But they thought he looked great during the physical exam. Then I helped a neighbor with some admin work they needed assistance with."

Chad gave her an admiring look. "In the last couple of days, you've rescued a dog from a negligent neighbor and solved another neighbor's issue with paperwork. I'd say you have this election in the bag."

"I wouldn't say that. I haven't been able to get around to see all the neighbors yet—most of them have no idea who I am. But it's a good start. I did also make it around to George Turner's house."

Chad frowned. "George Turner. Why is that name familiar?"

"He's the neighbor who died at the picnic."

"Oh, I remember now," said Chad. "And you went by his house?"

"Sorry, I'm really not trying to obfuscate. George, clearly, wasn't there. His son was at his house, clearing things out. I offered to give him a hand with sorting things, but he decided he'd rather take a break for a few minutes."

Chad said, "He's the one I met at the picnic. The surgeon, right?"

Sam nodded.

"Weren't you telling me that neighbors were gossiping about him? Something about him needing money from his father? Or having a bad relationship with his dad?"

"Yes. And you pointed out that Marcus was at the picnic, after all. That he was being supportive of his father, so things couldn't have been too awful between them," said Sam.

"Did he talk about the picnic at all?"

Sam said, "He did. He said he was there because his father wanted him there. That George wanted to show Marcus off to everyone."

Chad made a face. "So George wanted his successful surgeon son at the picnic to make himself look good."

"It sounded that way. Of course, from what Marcus was saying, it sounded like he and his dad had a relationship full of ups and downs. He did say that George wouldn't return his calls sometimes."

Chad said, "Did Marcus say anything about why there was some random mom giving his father CPR when he was the one with all the medical training?"

"Actually, he did. He said he froze up. Almost as if he was in shock."

Chad frowned. "Isn't medical training something almost like muscle memory? Wouldn't you spring into action when someone needed help?"

"It's probably different when it's your father. Anyway, George was basically the only parent George had. He said his mother had left the family when he was young. He doesn't seem to have a relationship with her at all."

Chad said, "And I thought *my* family was messed up."

"Your family *is* messed up," said Sam teasingly. "Just not as messed up as Marcus Turner's."

It was a quarter to six when Sam grabbed Mandy and Alfred's medical paperwork, put Arlo on a leash, and walked over to their house. The aim of the dog-walking-portion of the walk was to see how Arlo did on a leash, period. She'd carefully read online about introducing leashes to dogs and tried the loose leash walking technique where the owner rewards the dog every few paces with a treat when they don't pull on the leash. Arlo didn't seem to want to pull at all, happy to walk slightly in front of Sam. He definitely enjoyed the treats along the way.

The process took longer than Sam had thought. That was mainly because Arlo was very curious about the neighborhood he'd been living in, but had never really seen. She let him explore, sniff, and do lots of pottying.

Finally, they reached Mandy and Alfred's house. She tapped on the door and Alfred opened the door. A smile spread over his beefy face. "You've got Arlo!" He called for his wife and Mandy showed up right behind him. "Oh, you're making my day," she said with a smile. "That poor little baby."

Arlo gave them an engaging grin and wagged his tail hard to show how much he liked them. Sam gave him more treats.

"I wanted to give Arlo a little leash time, but I also wanted to let you know that I was able to take care of your billing issue today."

Mandy and Alfred looked at each other. "You mean you started the process? You actually got a representative on the phone who said they'd check on it for us?"

"No, I ended up going over there in person and waiting until I got confirmation it was handled." Sam pulled out the receipt of payment and the screenshot of their portal showing they owed nothing.

Mandy burst into tears. Alfred's own eyes welled up a little as he looked at the paperwork. "I don't know how you did it," he muttered.

"I have more time and flexibility than you do," Sam said. "That's all it is."

Mandy smiled and brushed her tears away with her hand. "Well, I think we'll vote for you for the HOA president."

"Heck, I'll vote for you for president of the US if you decide to run," said Alfred, still looking stunned. "Honestly, this is a huge, huge relief. We can't thank you enough."

"No thanks necessary," said Sam. "Your issue is the kind of thing that really burns me up. It makes me happy to bring it to a resolution. That's one reason today was a good day."

"Do you want to come in?" asked Alfred. "Have supper with us?"

Sam shook her head. "No, but thanks for asking. I have supper in the slow cooker at home, and I need to get Arlo back to the house. I'll see you soon, though."

And with that, Sam and Arlo headed back home. Sam believed Arlo had an extra spring to his step on the way back. She knew she did.

As usual, Sam was up bright and early on Tuesday morning. She fed Arlo, brushed his coat, and snuggled with him on the sofa while she drank her coffee and planned her day. Actually, it was more of a case of Sam checking her planner for the agenda she'd created the day before. It involved a visit to see Pris, the neighbor who'd hovered on the fringes of the picnic. She'd put a question mark next to the visit. She didn't want to cause any undue stress for Pris. But she was one of the last remaining people on her listening tour. Plus, high off her success with helping Mandy and Alfred, Sam was on the lookout for other people who might be able to use her assistance. If Pris had a hard time leaving her house, maybe she needed someone to run errands for her. It was a thought.

Sam considered the issue the entire time while she exercised after her coffee with Arlo. Arlo watched her adoringly as she lifted weights in their home gym, then hopped on the exercise bike. Perhaps it would be less stressful for Pris if Sam's visit seemed more like a random encounter. If she didn't knock on the door or ring the doorbell, it might be a little easier. Then she recalled Tuesday was trash day. Everyone was supposed to roll their bins out on the morning of collection day, instead of the night before. And it was prime time for the trash bins to be rolled out.

First, Sam rolled theirs out. Then she collected Arlo, put his red and black harness on him, gathered some poop bags, and headed out the door.

"You'll be an expert walker in no time," said Sam to Arlo. The dog beamed at her. "Plus, you look like a rockstar in that harness."

Arlo tossed his head in response, looking proud.

Sam looked Pris up in the directory before they left. On the way, they saw quite a few other neighbors putting their bins out. Each neighbor who saw Arlo with Sam looked first surprised and then delighted. A few of them reached out to pet Arlo, and he basked in their attention. One lady insisted on running inside the house and getting him a few treats.

"You'll be wanting to walk all day long, won't you?" Sam asked Arlo as they continued their trek to Pris's house. Arlo grinned up at her, his tongue hanging out the side of his mouth.

When they passed Arlo's old house, Arlo's ears drooped down, and he stopped short, a fearful expression on his face. Sam picked him up and walked briskly past the house. Arlo snuggled his head under her chin.

Pris's house was set back into the woods and barely visible from the street. There was a driveway that curved toward it, surrounded by heavy brush. To Sam's disappointment, there were no trash bins being trundled out to the street.

"Do you mind doing some extra walking?" Sam asked Arlo.

Arlo didn't.

So Sam took a rather circuitous route around a very short block. On the third trip around the block, Sam spotted some activity at the base of the driveway. "I think she's coming out," said Sam.

Arlo looked pleased at this. Although Arlo was looking pleased by just about everything.

Sam walked away from Pris's house, then turned around so that the timing would be good for Pris to meet her. It occurred to Sam that her behavior might constitute stalking, but the truth of the matter was that Sam's only goal was to be helpful, if she could. Stalkers rarely had their victim's best interests at heart. Encouraged by this thought, she continued on with her mission.

Pris deposited the trash bin at the side of the road. She was turning around and about to head back down her driveway when she saw Arlo and Sam and froze. Sam gave a cheerful smile. "Hi there!"

Pris looked back at the house as if she wanted to flee.

"I'm a new neighbor," said Sam. "Samantha Prescott, although everyone calls me Sam. It's good to meet you."

Pris reluctantly smiled back. "Nice to meet you. I'm Pris Lawrence."

"That's a beautiful name," said Sam. "And it's a lovely neighborhood, too. I know we'll enjoy Maple Hills."

Pris hesitated, clearly torn between escaping and continuing the conversation. "Welcome to the neighborhood," she said in a reserved voice. She glanced longingly back at her house.

In an attempt to put her at ease, Sam said, "I'm actually running for HOA president, by the way. I'm sure they'll be sending emails about it soon and probably including proxy vote information if you can't attend the meeting in person."

The mention of a meeting seemed to rattle Pris. She swallowed, looking again down her driveway. "Okay. That sounds good." Then she seemed to steel herself before turning back around with a shy smile. "I'll be sure to vote for you."

"Well, that's not the main reason I've been trying to speak with everyone in Maple Hills. I want to find out what everyone likes most about the subdivision and what they like the least. I'd love to make the neighborhood even better." Sam gave Pris her most earnest look.

Pris considered this. "You know, I can't think of anything right now. It all seems perfect to me."

"Most of the residents seem to want more activities," said Sam, curious to see Pris's reaction.

Pris recoiled. "No, I don't think that's something I'd like to see more of." She cast another look back at her house, as if she wished she were there.

Sam hesitated, then said, "I don't know if you need any help on a personal level at all, but that's something that always makes me happy. I can help run errands or manage household repairs, or bring over a meal. Any time at all."

Pris gave Sam a despairing look that Sam couldn't really understand. Was Pris the victim of some sort of abuse? Trapped in her life somehow? At any rate, Sam wasn't going to push any further.

Sam had come prepared with a piece of paper containing her name and phone number. It would have to do until she got the HOA secretary to send out an updated directory with her information on it.

"Call me. Anytime of the day or night. I'd be delighted to be an ear or to try to help in some way." She smiled at Pris. "Sorry to have held you up. I'd better take Arlo back home."

Pris said timidly, "He's a cute dog."

"Thanks! We're having fun together."

Arlo rewarded Sam with a smile. They headed off, Sam giving Pris a wave as she left. She mentally ran through a list of reasons Pris might be in such a state. Was she experiencing a mental health challenge of some kind? Agoraphobia had come to mind, but perhaps there was something else. Or maybe it was some other sort of health issue that she preferred to keep private. A chronic illness maybe. Or maybe she was simply shy and withdrawn. Or using her home as a place to follow her creative pursuits. Sam felt her usual need to try to fix things, coupled with the realization that she didn't need to overstep and make Pris feel even more stressed out than she already did. It was a quandary for Sam, who usually wanted to swoop in right away. But perhaps Pris didn't really need or want help. Perhaps she was satisfied with her life the way that it was. Sam told herself sternly that she needed not to see problems where there really weren't any.

On the way home, there was another neighbor putting out his bins. He was one of the ones on her list for the listening tour. Luckily, he wasn't hurrying back inside. Instead, he had a broom and was sweeping off his front walk. He was a tall man with broad shoulders and tousled black hair.

"Hi there," said Sam as she approached with Arlo. "Good morning."

The man gave her a slow smile. "Good morning," he said, as he pushed his hair out of his eyes. "You must be the new neighbor I've been hearing about."

Sam grimaced. "Uh-oh. That sounds ominous."

"Not at all. Everyone seems delighted to have you in Maple Hills. Plus, there's talk about you running for HOA president."

"I'm afraid so," said Sam breezily. "I like to help out." Which was a tremendous understatement. "I'm Samantha Prescott. Everyone calls me Sam."

He gave her that lazy smile again. "I'm Aiden Wood. Everyone calls me Aiden." He nodded to Arlo, who was eagerly pulling at the leash for Aiden to pet him. "I recognize this little guy. You're a hero to everyone in the neighborhood, you know.

I can't tell you how many times I wanted to do the same thing." He scratched Arlo behind his ears and Arlo's eyes closed blissfully.

"I couldn't stand it," said Sam. "I couldn't drive or walk by the house with him chained up like that. The owner seemed happy to let me have him, so we both benefitted."

"That's a generous way of looking at it," said Aiden, a smile tugging at his lips.

"It's the truth. It was a win-win situation."

"How are you enjoying Maple Hills so far?" asked Aiden. He stopped, frowning. "You weren't at the picnic, were you?"

"I'm afraid I was. Were you?"

Aiden shook his head. "I sat that one out. I've been to a few picnics and sometimes they ended up being sort of stressful. You know how neighbors can be."

"I do. Although usually it just extends to carping about Christmas decorations that stay up too long or yardwork that needs to be done. Murder is a little outside the norm."

Aiden was still. "You think it was murder?"

"Don't you? It sounds as if George Turner had upset quite a few people in the neighborhood. The police were on the scene getting witness statements. And George was in the habit of bringing his own food to any neighborhood gatherings. If an allergen was in his food, it was placed there by someone at the picnic."

Aiden gave her an appraising look. "That's all true. Very astute."

Sam was pleased, but gave a shrug to hide the fact. "His death didn't make sense otherwise." She tilted her head, looking thoughtfully at Aiden. "And now my astuteness is giving me the feeling that you know more than you're letting on about all this."

Aiden stopped petting Arlo and Arlo gave him a gentle bump with his head to encourage him to keep going. "You pick up on a lot."

Sam shrugged again. "I'm good at reading body language."

Aiden said slowly, "I formerly worked at the Sunset Ridge police department. I used to be a detective there."

Sam raised her eyebrows. "So you *do* know more."

He seemed to be weighing whether or not to fill her in. Sizing her up. After a moment, he said, "I don't know very much, but I did get a little information from some old buddies at the station. It would be something you'd need to keep quiet."

Sam smiled at him. "Keeping quiet is one of my specialties."

He gave her a doubtful look, but if he'd known her better, he wouldn't have been concerned. Sam kept secrets like Fort Knox kept gold. If someone told her something in confidence, she'd never say anything to anybody. But if they *didn't*, that was a whole other story.

Aiden said, "From what I heard, it's definitely a suspicious death. Mostly for the reasons you listed."

"Did you hear anything about what the motive might be?"

"All they could tell me is that there were plenty of people who weren't happy with George Turner," said Aiden. "Naturally, the cops wanted to speak with me too, since I was a neighbor."

Sam raised her eyebrows. "Even though you weren't at the picnic?"

"Mostly because they wanted my take on George, I think."

"What *was* your take on him?" asked Sam.

He gave her a considering look again. "That he was the kind of person who was used to getting his own way. That he enjoyed being in control, or having the illusion of being in control. Control is a very nebulous thing."

Sam said, "Yes, it can be. I'll admit to having some control freak tendencies. It really puts my nose out of joint when things are completely outside my control." She paused. "There are a few neighbors who seemed especially upset with George."

He chuckled. "It sounds like you've figured out a lot about Maple Hills's dynamics, considering you're brand-new here."

"I try," said Sam. "Do you think you could corroborate the suspects I've come up with?"

"Now you sound like a reporter."

"Do I?" asked Sam, beaming. "That's a career that's always interested me."

"To answer your question, if you list the people, I'll see what I think."

"Okay," said Sam. Then she frowned. "Wait. You don't have any relatives or close friends here, do you? I don't want to create an awkward situation."

"No worries on that score," said Aiden. He leaned on his broom.

"Okay. Well, first up is Julia Harper. I understand she and George Turner had issues dating back to a park revitalization project that they both worked on. And that their issues might have spilled over into the neighborhood, as well."

Aiden looked less lazy and more focused now. He nodded. "I think you've got a good take on that."

Samantha gave him a pleased smile. She decided not to mention Olivia, since she'd promised to keep her secret affair with George under wraps. "Marcus Turner, George's son. I hear he might have some financial issues and a history of bad feelings between the two of them."

Aiden nodded. "Family members are often suspects. I think Marcus might have had a motive to murder."

"Sad, but true. Next up, I have someone I'm not sure should even be on the list. Nora Snodwick."

Aiden grinned again. "Yes, I know who she is. She can be a real rabble-rouser in Maple Hills sometimes."

"She seemed pretty aggravated that her plan to start up a community watch program was stymied by George. I got the impression that they weren't the closest of next-door neighbors."

"Well, that's an understatement," said Aiden with a laugh. "There's no love lost there. I'd say she should *definitely* be on your suspect list. After all, it wouldn't take any strength to murder someone with an allergen. And I've been to a few HOA meetings where I thought Nora might want to murder George right then and there."

"Got it," said Sam. "Maybe I should speak with Nora next. I talked to her at the picnic, but I didn't get too much information about her relationship with George." She paused. "Out of curiosity, or just plain nosiness, what are you doing now that you've left the police force?" She blushed a little. "Of course, there's no rule that you have to be doing anything at all. I'm not working, myself."

Aiden's gaze focused on her again. "Stay-at-home mom?" he asked casually.

"Hmm? Oh, no. No children." She didn't delve into the widget thing, since it always seemed complicated to explain to anyone who asked questions. Besides, she was more interested in what Aiden was doing.

"I'm a teacher at the high school now," he said. "I was ready for something completely different after working with the police. And before you ask, the kids have a day off today."

Sam considered this. "Was working as a detective here discouraging? Sorry for all the questions; you don't have to answer them if you don't want to. It's just that I was hoping Sunset Ridge didn't have a dark, criminal underbelly."

That made him laugh out loud. "No, it really doesn't. But still, there was enough going on that made me lose my faith in humanity a little. With teaching, I thought maybe I'd have a shot at influencing young minds more positively. Stop someone from heading in the wrong direction at the beginning of the process instead of at the end. When you're always arresting people, you can't help but think things could have been different if they'd had a role model earlier." He waved his hand dismissively. "I'm not saying I'm the perfect role model, but I'm better than some."

"I bet you are," said Sam. "What subject do you teach?"

"Technology. It's pretty fun, actually. The kids really like the subject and I try to make it as entertaining as I can. It's been a good career change."

Sam said, "That's really cool. It's got to feel like a rewarding job after being a police officer." She glanced at her watch. "I should head back to the house. Arlo might need water after the length of this walk. Nice meeting you."

"Nice meeting you, too."

Chapter Nine

Arlo did indeed need water and guzzled quite a bit of it. Then he curled up on his bed for a nap, snoring enthusiastically while Sam tidied up. After tidying up inside, she moved into the yard for a little yard work. The yard service did a good job, but there were definitely weeds that could use pulling. She felt it made more sense to pull them on the edges of the property first, since those were the areas people could see. She walked down near the street, holding a plastic bucket and gardening gloves.

The weeds were well-entrenched, which made Sam even more determined to yank the interlopers out of the ground. She hadn't realized going in that she'd be engaging in such aerobic activity or she'd have worn breathable clothing. Despite it being September in the North Carolina mountains, it was decidedly warm.

On a particularly vigorous yank, she ended up falling backwards when the stubborn weed finally gave up. She was sitting flat on the lawn, looking very surprised, when she found Nora Snodwick staring at her from the road with a mixture of amusement and concern on her face.

"You okay?" she asked. "You didn't break your tailbone, did you?"

Sam delicately stood up. "No, nothing seems to be broken." She glared down at the offending weeds. "These things are tough to pull up." She looked back at Nora, who was walking a pit bull wearing a pink tutu, who was also observing her with interest. "I didn't know you had a dog. May I pet her?"

"Him," said Nora with a sniff. "And you may. Let Precious smell you first, to get acquainted."

Precious wagged his tail at her encouragingly when Sam offered the back of her hand for a sniff. Then she petted him. "Cute guy."

"He is, isn't he?" said Nora proudly. "Can you believe there was an active effort to ban him from the neighborhood?"

"Really?" That seemed overstepping, even for an HOA. "Were there any problems with neighbors or something like that?"

"Of course not," snapped Nora. "Precious is always perfectly behaved. I wish I could say the same for other dogs in Maple Hills. The campaign was spearheaded by George Turner. I believed at the time he'd done it simply to be mean and get back at me."

This was precisely the type of information that Sam was looking for. "Oh? Why would he do something like that?"

"Because that's the kind of man he was. He added a section to the HOA bylaws that would state dog breed restrictions. Pit bulls were to be included. Can you imagine?"

Sam said slowly, "That seems very directed at you. There wouldn't have been any grandfathering?"

Nora shook her head angrily.

"What precipitated the whole issue?"

Nora frowned at her. "If you're asking why he did it, it was because he was trying to get back at me, I'm sure. But the things *I* was complaining about were completely reasonable."

Sam scratched Precious behind the ears, and Precious grinned happily. "What kinds of things were you complaining about?"

"Well, there were a few. I did bring up at an HOA meeting that the entrance to Maple Hills needed a new landscaper. I thought George's pick was sloppy, and the landscaping was uninspired. The guy was doing the bare minimum of work. He'd throw a few pansies in the mix over the winter, and that would be it. He apparently disliked trimming bushes, because they were always scraggly looking."

Sam asked, "What were some of the other ones?" Nora narrowed her eyes at her and Sam explained, "I'm definitely running for president of the HOA. This helps me think ahead."

Nora launched into some of the other issues she'd noticed in the neighborhood. "George didn't do a good job following up on flagrant violations of the bylaws. People were doing all sorts of things. Grass was growing through cracks in the driveways. Trash bins were being left at the roadside until the following day. It was quite a mess."

"I'm surprised to hear that. My impression was that George was unpopular precisely because he took the HOA seriously."

Nora said, "Oh, he took it seriously. But he was more interested in other areas of control with the HOA. Architectural review, for one. The day-to-day drudgery of stomping out violations was tiresome for him. What we all hated most was his attitude. George liked to lord it over us at the meetings. And he wouldn't let me speak! He'd constantly interrupt me during meetings, dismissing my proposals before I could even fully present them. Or, if I *was* able to get an entire couple of sentences out, he'd publicly criticize my ideas or belittle them." Nora looked as steamed now as she must have felt during the meetings. Precious gave her a worried look, and Nora gave him an absentminded rub.

"It sounds like he was very condescending. That must have been very frustrating."

Nora gave a short laugh. "Frustrating isn't the word. It was infuriating. He undermined me at every opportunity. George also didn't follow protocol. He'd make decisions about Maple Hills improvements without putting them through a vote. He'd talk about neighborhood business with a select group of residents, which directly violated the rules."

Sam nodded. "His behavior sounds awful. But it doesn't really explain why he wanted to target you and Precious."

Precious continued looking anxious at the tone of the two humans.

Nora pursed her lips as if not really wanting to disclose the reasons she and George were engaged in a vendetta. She finally reluctantly said, "I suppose it all started when George himself started breaking the rules. Maybe he thought the HOA rules didn't apply to him because he was the president. But it was all very annoying."

"What types of rules was he breaking?"

"It started with his untrimmed bushes. They were eyesores, Sam. I believe he left them untrimmed just to spite me. You know I live next door to him."

Sam nodded.

"His fence was an issue, too. I measured it and it was taller than what was allowed by the HOA. But George wouldn't even listen to me when I complained about it. I mean, why even have bylaws if they're completely meaningless? What's the point?"

"I see," said Sam. "So George wasn't a stickler for following the rules."

"Not a bit. He also had paint splatters on his driveway from some home improvement project he was working on. Plus, he could be very noisy. I'd have to complain to him about that, too."

"I see," said Sam again. And she did. She saw Nora was clearly behaving like a pest. She hadn't liked the way George was treating her at the HOA meetings and had retaliated in her own way.

"Worst of all was that George was spreading rumors about me. I simply couldn't have that, of course. The very idea." Nora looked even more steamed than she had been.

"What type of rumors?" Sam's imagination was running wild. Did Nora have a secret life?

"He said all sorts of nonsense, probably to see if any of it would stick. He told people my memory was getting addled, that I couldn't handle responsibility, that I was financially insecure." She gritted her teeth. "It all made me furious."

"Understandably so."

Nora suddenly seemed to remember that she was speaking ill of the dead. Not only that, but someone whose death was being investigated as a potential murder. She added mildly, "Of course, I can't pretend to be brokenhearted over George's death. But I had nothing to do with it. Nothing." She paused and a look of pride passed across her features. "However, the police seem to think I could be a potential suspect. Me! At my age. It feels almost like a compliment. Maybe they consider me dangerous. They asked how close I was to George at the picnic. Close to George *and* his food, I suppose. I told them I was fairly close to him once, early on, mostly to tell him off."

"Understandably," said Sam.

Nora sniffed again. "Anyway, it wouldn't have been my style to murder George. I'd have gotten a lot more satisfaction out of making his life miserable. I'd have played loud Sinatra songs all hours of the day and night. It's much more fun to draw things out, don't you think so?"

"I can see where that would be more satisfying." Precious beamed at Sam as if happy she understood what his mama was saying.

Nora said, "I've been thinking over who might have done this, of course. I'm an old woman with little to do. Of course, you got some of my first impressions at the picnic."

"You mentioned Julia Harper, I believe."

Nora said, "You have an excellent memory, my dear. Yes, indeed. But Julia was perhaps more of an obvious choice. When I got back home, I started thinking more about Olivia Stanton."

Sam was certainly not going to disclose what she knew about Olivia and George's affair to the gossipy Nora. But she was happy to play dumb and see what Nora knew. "Really? I met Olivia recently. She seems like a nice woman."

Nora gave a surly snort. "Well, of course she *seems* nice. Everyone at the picnic *seemed* nice. That's how they'll try to get away with murder. Anyway, at my age, I have the luxury of hanging out on my back deck all day with Precious. We like to watch life go by, don't we, boy?"

Precious wagged his tail enthusiastically, shaking the pink tutu about as he did.

"I happen to have the perfect view of George's backyard. He appeared to think he was being private there because of a few trees. However, he was always in full view. I can also see Olivia's backyard from my deck."

"She lives next door?" asked Sam, frowning. She'd spoken to so many people in the last week and done so much walking that she was getting a bit confused over the layout of the neighborhood. She hadn't thought Olivia and Nora were next to each other, though.

"No, her backyard is adjacent to mine. A corner touches it. So let's say I've seen a lot of sneaking around when Olivia's husband isn't around." She sniffed.

"You think George and Olivia were . . . ?"

"Naturally." Nora pursed her lips. "Although I'm actually very fond of Olivia. She seems like a very nice young woman. I'm much more furious with George. I've absolutely no doubt that he was the one tempting Olivia to go astray. Hateful beast of a man." She gave Sam a menacing look through beady eyes. "I don't want this information to go any further, understand? Perhaps I shouldn't have told you about it, but you have kind eyes."

Sam blinked her kind eyes in surprise. "I won't say a word."

"Good. Not because I care a lick about what anybody thinks of George Turner. But I do care what people think about Olivia. I'm rather fond of her. I'm not saying Olivia isn't flighty and distracted, because she is. But I still do like her. If the gossip spreads, I'll know who started it," she said darkly, glaring at Sam. Then she tilted her head to one side. "Onto other matters. You're running for the open president spot. What's your strategy?"

Sam paused. She definitely didn't want to make an enemy of Nora. "You're absolutely sure that *you're* not interested in running for it?"

"Heavens, no. I'm far too old for that. I'd like to have someone in the office who actually listens to me. I don't ask for much. And you've done an excellent job at listening to me for the last fifteen minutes."

"Okay. I've completed my listening tour where I've surveyed neighbors on what they most like about Maple Hills and what they'd most like to change."

Nora raised her penciled-on eyebrows. "Clever. That way you introduce yourself, tell people you're running, and offer them hope their concerns will be addressed. Yes, that's quite smart."

Precious lolled his tongue out in agreement.

"I do have signs I need to put around a couple of spots in the neighborhood. My yard, of course, but also near the entrance and maybe in the common areas. I should pick those up from the printer, actually."

Nora scowled at her. "Time's a-wasting," she said. "You'd better hop to it. I read the bylaws and I know that election needs to be held without delay. If I were you, I'd stop weeding and go run that errand."

"I'll do that," said Sam meekly.

Nora tilted her head to one side. "Happy to hear it." She paused. "During your tour, did you meet a little dog named Arlo? The poor creature was chained to the front yard and has disappeared. I fear something horrible has happened to him. Precious and I were always so devastated when we walked by his house. I had words with the owner *several* times. A very hard-headed man. Now, if *he* had been murdered, I'd most certainly have been a suspect."

Sam said, "Oh, I have good news about Arlo. I took him home with me."

Now it was Nora's turn to blink in surprise. "Did you? How? Did you kidnap him?"

"I thought about it. But then I thought it was easier to ask the owner. I pointed out that it would solve his problem since it was clear he didn't want his dog. There might have been a bit of pressure applied. In the end, the owner surrendered Arlo."

Nora gave Sam an admiring look. "How is he doing? I'd think it would be tough for him to acclimate to a big house after being in a small yard for so long. His world suddenly expanded tremendously."

"That was a worry of mine, too. But he's adapting really well so far. He's even been doing great on the leash."

Nora nodded with satisfaction. "He's a smart little thing, I'll give you that." She glanced down at Precious, who wagged his tail again. "Precious and I should continue on our way. If you need any help campaigning, let me know. I'll put the word out." And Nora ambled away.

If Nora was going to help Sam win the spot, Sam decided she should work on one of Nora's priorities first. So after she went inside the house, she looked into what it would take to set up a neighborhood watch in Maple Hills. Then she emailed Nora to see if she would have any interest in being a captain for the program.

While she was in her inbox, she saw the HOA vice president, Hank, had emailed her back regarding the run. He'd been as discouraging as possible, listing the long hours required by the position, the thankless work, and his suspicion that Sam didn't have her finger on the pulse of Maple Ridge because she'd just moved in. At the end of the email, though, he grudgingly admitted that he could not stop her from running, although he warned her not to be disappointed when she didn't get any votes. Sam decided it was just as well that she'd left Hank off of her listening tour. Apparently, he hadn't heard about her approach. Perhaps she was catching him off guard.

Then she heeded Nora's advice and set off for the sign making business to pick up her campaign signs. She was eager to see how they'd all turned out, considering she'd labored over the decision for the slogan. She'd tossed around about twenty different ideas in her head. Chad had been very patient with her for about the first two hours, then told her that "Choose Sam, Choose Change," "Prescott: Your Voice, Your Choice," or "Prescott for Progress" would all do nicely.

And, when the owner gave her one of the signs to review, she had to admit that "Prescott for Progress" looked good on the sign. She'd originally planned *not* to include a picture, but was worried no one would know who she was otherwise, despite her listening tour. People were so very busy these days that her name might have gone in one ear and out through the other. Once back in Maple Hills, she planted a few signs. Then she checked her email and saw that not only had Nora accepted her future role as neighborhood watch captain, she'd also invited Sam to put a campaign sign in her yard, which Sam quickly followed through on.

When she came back inside, Arlo wagged his tail enthusiastically and licked her hand when she reached down to rub him.

"Out conquering the world?" asked Chad, muting a baseball game on the TV.

"No, it was more of an attempt to conquer Maple Hills."

Chad raised an eyebrow. "You put the signs up? How did they turn out?"

Sam showed him a picture of one sign that she'd taken with her phone.

"Wow, they turned out great," he said. "When is the election?"

"I got an email a few minutes ago from the Maple Hills HOA secretary. She said she'd email the ballots in a couple of days. Then we need to allow time for everyone to send them back and for them to be counted, of course."

"Naturally. Well, I'm sure you're a shoo-in. Didn't you tell me there was another likely candidate?"

"Hank. He emailed me earlier, trying to discourage me from running. He's the vice-president now and apparently as unpopular as George Turner was. I got the impression from various neighbors that he's on a perpetual power trip."

Chad tsked. "Not the smartest thing to do if you want to win an election."

"I guess he didn't think it through all the way. Or else he thought he'd always be the number two man behind George Turner."

Chad said, "Well, you went about things the right way. The listening tour was genius. And the signs look amazing."

"Oh, and I also sent out an introductory email explaining my platform, my background, and asking for votes. I told our neighbors to reach out to me if they needed help with anything at all."

Chad's eyes grew wide. "Did you? Isn't that a little dangerous?"

"I doubt it. It's the kind of thing that you say and that people appreciate, but never really ask you to do anything."

"Let's hope," said Chad.

Chapter Ten

It was early Wednesday morning when there was a timid knock on the front door. Arlo looked surprised, then started barking. His own barking seemed to surprise him even more than the knock did.

Sam was sitting in the sunroom at the time and was glad she was appropriately attired in exercise gear rather than pajamas, despite the early hour. She peered out the window and didn't immediately see anyone. She craned her head more and saw a small child, weeping on her doorstep.

Sam yanked open the door. "Whatever is the matter? Are you okay?"

The little boy shook his head, wiping his nose with the back of his hand. "I missed the bus."

Sam's mind whirled. She wasn't entirely sure why the missed bus resulted in the little boy on her doorstep, but she was happy to invite him in, offer him a tissue, learn his name, and find out how to help him.

Fortunately, he settled down almost immediately, looking curiously around him at the big house. His mouth opened in an

O when he spotted Arlo. Arlo wagged his tail at him, his tongue lolling out amiably.

"Did you steal that dog?" asked the boy.

"What? No, I don't steal. The owner gave him to me."

"Why?" asked the boy.

"Because he had a hard time taking care of him. But let's talk about how to take care of you. What's your name?"

"Franklin."

"Last name?" asked Sam.

"Smith."

Sam nodded. "Okay. I seem to remember a couple of Smiths in Maple Hills. Which family do you belong with?"

Franklin filled her in and she pulled up the HOA directory on her phone.

"What are you doing?" asked Franklin apprehensively.

"Well, I'm calling your folks. I don't want anyone to think I've kidnapped you."

Franklin frowned. "That's not a very good idea. My parents are both at work. They have lots of meetings, so it's bad to interrupt them."

"I think they should know you missed the bus," said Sam, feeling as if she was losing control of the situation. Although she hadn't really had a handle on it even from the start.

"Definitely not," said Franklin. "They'll just get mad." He picked up a tug toy from Arlo's extensive toy basket, and Arlo started enthusiastically playing with him.

"How did you end up at my house?" asked Sam, still puzzled how her morning had suddenly gotten so out of control.

"Your signs," said Franklin. "They said you'd help."

Sam rubbed her temples. Chad was right. That had been a bad idea.

"I'd asked Mom who you were yesterday when I saw the signs. She told me you lived in the big house. This is the only huge house around." Franklin shrugged.

"Okay, that makes sense, I guess. But you can't stay here playing with Arlo all day."

Arlo looked disappointed to hear this.

"I'll drive you to school. Which one is it?"

Franklin filled her in as to the correct elementary school. When asked if he was hungry, he nodded, so Sam found him some yogurt and fruit. While he was eating, she did text both parents, called the school, and also gave the local police a heads-up. The last thing she needed was for the police to pull her over when she had someone else's kid in the car.

The father didn't answer her back, but the mother did immediately. She was very apologetic and thanked Sam for helping her out. Thankfully, she also gave Sam explicit permission to drive her child to school, which made Sam worry less about ending up in jail during the errand.

When she returned to the house, she spent a little time resuming the tug game with Arlo. He was delighted to play while she considered the day ahead of her. Maybe she'd finish the weeding she'd started yesterday. She definitely wanted to check in with the HOA secretary to see if there was anything else she needed to do to make sure she was on the ballot. There were a couple of other odds and ends, including cooking supper, that she should attend to as well.

Chad was up fairly early for him. "Everything okay?" he asked with a yawn, clearly expecting a yes.

"I suppose so."

Chad looked more focused and awake. "Uh-oh. That doesn't sound good. What happened?"

"As much as it pains me, you might have been right about my offer to help. A little boy named Franklin ended up at our front door because he'd missed the bus and needed a ride to his elementary school."

Chad snorted. "Oh, no."

"Oh, yes. He was a pleasant little guy, but I kept thinking I was going to be arrested for kidnapping. It was very disconcerting."

Chad said, "It's not too late to delete the part about helping."

"No, I think it's probably too late by now. The election is upon us. And if I send another email out, rescinding my offer of helping, it makes me look wishy-washy. Or like I really don't want to help, after all."

Chad sighed. "You're right. Well, maybe that will be the only thing that comes of it. What have you got on your agenda for today? I think I'm going to run to the hardware store in a few minutes."

Sam listed the things she'd put on her schedule. It was a surprisingly light day for her. "It feels as if there's something I'm missing," she said.

Chad leaned over and gave her a light kiss. "Nothing is missing. Think of it as you paving the way for some serendipity to happen in your life. When everything is planned out too much, you don't have any room for spontaneity. What's the saying? *Life is what happens when you're busy making other plans?*"

"True," Sam acknowledged.

Chad said carefully, in the kind of voice that wants to avoid causing offense, "I always worry about you, you know. You have such a tough time sitting still and relaxing. You're always on the go, always checking your lists or making new ones. You never make time for yourself."

Sam nodded slowly. The problem was, and the thing that was so hard to explain, was that staying on the go *was* time for herself. That relaxing just seemed to make her brain even busier. "I know it's something I've got to work on," she said instead.

Then the doorbell rang.

They looked at each other. "Did you have any home repairs scheduled today? Plumber, HVAC, etc.?" asked Chad.

"Nothing. I guess it's serendipity once again," said Sam, sounding a little sour. She was the kind of person who preferred things running according to plan. This particular day had gone completely haywire.

Chad peered out the window next to the door. He slowly opened it to Pris Lawrence, who appeared startled to see him.

"Pris," said Sam quickly. Chad seemed to register Pris's dismay because he smiled pleasantly at Pris before disappearing into the cavernous basement.

Pris looked as if she was in an agony of indecision. Or as if she might bolt away from the house at any second. "I didn't mean to bother you," she said in a gruff voice.

"You're not bothering me a bit," said Sam, falling effortlessly back into hostess mode. "Come on in. I was about to pour myself a cup of coffee—can I get you one?"

Pris nodded shyly, looking around her.

Arlo also seemed shy. He bolted under an end table, watching Pris carefully.

"Take a seat anywhere," called Sam from the kitchen. "I'll join you in two shakes."

Pris continued looking around her, hesitant, as if choosing the right location in which to sit was some sort of test. Finally, she settled in a velvety navy-blue armchair in the corner of the tastefully decorated living room. She sat very straight, almost at attention. And her expression still indicated that she could make an excuse and disappear at any time.

Sam handed her a cup and saucer and said, "Cream? Sugar?"

"Both, please," said Pris, unable to meet Sam's gaze.

Sam doctored Pris's coffee, then sat across from her in a similar armchair. "What a delightful surprise," said Sam. "I love it when people have coffee with me. It makes me feel less indulgent for being on my third cup." She paused, studying Pris's face. "But am I right in thinking everything is not well with you?"

Pris looked down at her cup and saucer. Her hair fell in a curtain so Sam couldn't read her features. "I . . . well, I don't know really what to say." She suddenly sat up straight again. "I shouldn't be here."

"Oh, I hope you won't leave. Is there something I can do for you?" Sam reached down and snapped her fingers at Arlo, who was still hovering under the end table. He ran, still crouched over, and Sam scooped him up and put him in her lap.

Pris looked up shyly and then down again. "Thank you. Getting help is exactly the reason I'm here right now."

Sam decided she was really going to have to spend more time heeding Chad's advice. She'd perfected the art of looking as if she was listening closely before doing precisely what she wanted to. But he was right about the offer to help. If it was going to be like this all day, she'd be in hot water. She sat quietly, waiting for Pris to elaborate on the reason for her visit. Arlo leaned against her chest, watching Pris apprehensively.

Finally, Pris said, "I'm worried, that's what my problem is. Worried, and I have no one to really talk to." Her mouth twisted a little. "Of course, I don't have anyone but myself to blame for that."

"I don't think you should blame yourself for anything at all. I'm glad you're here. And I'm happy to hear anything you have to say."

Sam and Pris sat in companionable quiet for a few moments while Pris appeared to be gathering her thoughts. "The police have been talking to me. And that really worries me."

"The police? Regarding George Turner's death?" Sam frowned. "But everyone realized you had nothing to do with that. You were nowhere near George."

"True, but they're not sure that's really the case." Pris rubbed her face, looking tired. "They said witnesses told them that George was moving around a good deal early on at the picnic and could have been around me for a few seconds at the beginning. He wasn't, but the police didn't seem interested in hearing the truth. I wish I'd never gone to that picnic."

Sam said slowly, "If I can ask, what made you finally decide to go?"

Pris thought about this for a few moments. "Mostly a sense of obligation. I'd avoided most opportunities to get together with the neighbors. I felt like I *should* go. I was also a little curious about the events. And maybe I felt like I wanted to have a normal life for once."

"You don't think you have a normal life now?"

Pris gave a short laugh. "No. A normal life is when someone leaves home and interacts with the community. Sees friends. Goes to coffees."

"We're having a coffee now," said Sam cheerfully. She didn't want to push Pris.

Pris rewarded her with a small smile. "True. I've been really reluctant to reach out to people in Maple Hills. In my last neighborhood, the atmosphere there was really toxic. It was the last thing I wanted to repeat. The neighbors were at each other's throats all the time, arguing about property lines, lawn heights, and trash bins. I decided when I moved here that I'd stay out of all that." She shrugged, looking tired. "But it didn't work out the way I thought it would. Now all the neighbors think I'm a recluse or something."

"So you're *wanting* to spend more time with them?"

Pris nodded. "I think so. It's hard to say because being in groups stresses me out so much. Maybe if I take things a little bit at a time."

"That sounds like a smart approach. You can always back off if things get to be too much." Sam paused. "I'll admit I'm really confused about the police interest in you."

Pris buried her face in her hands. A sob escaped, and Sam carefully set down Arlo and hurried off to find a box of tissues.

"Thanks," muttered Pris as she took them from her. She took a deep, shuddering breath. "Please don't say anything about this. I'm so ashamed."

"I won't say a word."

Pris nodded. "Okay. I have a past record. The police knew about it. It's a DWI. I made a terrible mistake one night. I was at home and had a couple of glasses of wine. I'd killed the bottle, so I headed out to the store and buy another one. I was pulled over on the way."

Sam winced.

"Yeah. I don't know what I was thinking. It was a sign to me I needed to stop drinking. I never really thought I had a problem until that moment. I'm so glad no one else was hurt. I think about it every day. At least something good came out of it when I quit alcohol."

Sam said, "That's true. But why would the police think the DWI had anything to do with George Turner's death?"

Pris took a deep breath. "It's because George knew about it. That's another reason I didn't want to go to Maple Hills events—I wanted to avoid him. I was terrified he'd tell everyone about me . . . about my worst day. That everyone would judge me."

"How did George know about it?"

Pris shrugged. "He said he'd dug into my background. I don't know why he did it. Maybe it's something he did whenever anyone new moved into the neighborhood. I got the impression that he enjoyed having something to hold over people. Something that could function as a stick or a carrot."

"Control," said Sam, nodding. "He wanted control." Sam understood this completely. It was one of those things she struggled with herself. She was horrible at delegating and knew her first thought was always that she'd likely do a more careful job than anyone else. It had been her New Year's resolution to work on for the past five or six years.

Pris said, "He did. Even worse than that, he wanted me to pay him to keep quiet."

"Blackmail." Sam felt a rising tide of anger.

"That's right. But I don't have a lot of extra cash. I'd paid so much for a lawyer to help with the DWI. Then I put myself in rehab to help stop drinking. After that, I put the rest of my money into this house, since I thought I'd never really feel secure until I had a place I could afford."

"I totally understand that," said Sam. "So what happened? What did you tell George?"

Pris gave another unhappy laugh. "I told him I needed time to raise the money. But it was going to take me forever to get it. The thing that upset me the most is that George didn't even need the money. So now the police think I murdered George because he was blackmailing me."

"How did they find out about that?"

Pris said in a low voice, "They took his laptop and found out he'd been emailing me. Extorting me."

"That doesn't sound like a very smart method of blackmailing someone." Sam, always someone with an eye to the efficient, thought there were many other, better ways of accomplishing the blackmail. Meeting in person or leaving envelopes with typed missives seemed a lot better.

"True," said Pris with a smile. "But then, I guess George never dreamed he'd be caught."

"That was careless of him. As far as he knew, you might have been the type of person to turn him over to the cops for blackmail. After all, it wasn't as if the police didn't know about your DWI."

Pris said, "Yes, but the idea of everyone gossiping about me kept me quiet. Anyway, George said he had a lot of influence at the police department and they'd never charge him. He did some kind of fundraiser for the police charity."

"Okay. It sounds like the best thing to do is to focus the police's attention elsewhere. I know you have had limited contact with our neighbors, but is there anyone who stands out as a suspect?"

Pris recoiled. "Oh, I'd rather not say."

"So there is someone," said Sam. "I'm not going to tell anyone. I just want to explore the possibility."

Pris said slowly, "I guess I'd have to say Nora. Have you met her?"

"Yes, a couple of times. She seems like the kind of person who really knows what's happening in the neighborhood."

Pris gave a wry smile. "That's one way of putting it. I hate to even think she could be involved in George's death. Nora's actually been very kind to me."

This surprised Sam. Of all the words used to describe Nora, "kind" wasn't the first to come to mind.

Pris said, "I haven't wanted to attend the HOA meetings, but I was interested in finding out everything that was covered. I'd like to try to be a good neighbor, even though I'm dealing with some personal challenges."

Pris didn't explain the challenges, and Sam didn't ask.

Pris continued, "Nora taped the meetings for me and emailed me the link. I don't even know how she figured out how to do it, since she said she was awful with technology. But it helped me feel like I was part of the group."

"That *was* kind of her," said Sam. "But she's obviously had some run-ins with George."

Pris looked relieved that she didn't have to spell it out. "You've heard. Good."

"It sounded like she's been unhappy with the way George ran the HOA. Plus, she mentioned that he'd spread rumors about her."

Pris nodded. "She complained about George a lot in the emails she sent me. The emails were basically rants with a link attached."

The door opened, and Chad came in, whistling. Pris jumped, and Sam sighed. Whatever further information she might have gotten was now lost as Pris scrambled to her feet. "I'm sorry," she said breathlessly. "I've held you up for too long. Thanks for the coffee."

Chad finally seemed to realize they still had a guest. He put down the bags he was carrying and started walking over to Pris to greet her. But she gave them both an apologetic look and scurried out the door. Arlo watched her go from across the room.

Chapter Eleven

"Wow," said Chad. "Am I scary-looking?"

"No, she's just easily startled. Skittish."

Chad started putting the groceries away. "Which neighbor is this? They're starting to run together."

"Not one you met at the picnic, for sure. She's Pris Lawrence, and she's a major introvert. Or shy. Or possibly both. At any rate, she's not fond of gatherings, although she steeled herself to attend the picnic."

Chad frowned. "Yeah, I don't remember her."

"She stayed on the edges of the group the whole time, but she left early. I think she might have even left before George Turner died."

Chad said, "How did you convince her to come over for a coffee?" He glanced over into the sunroom where the two cups still sat.

"I didn't, actually. She came over here. I'd met her while walking Arlo and told her I could be an ear. At least, I think that's what I said. Anyway, she's been alarmed about the police asking her questions and wanted to chat about it."

Chad snorted. “It sounds like she’s the only one who definitely *didn’t* do it. As usual, the cops point in totally the wrong direction.”

“I’m sure they’re simply following protocol and being careful.”

Chad said, “Did she seem better after telling you about it? I didn’t get much of an impression from her except her determination to get as far away from me as possible.”

“Who knows? Maybe she felt a little better. I hope so.”

Chad said, “What’s your plan for helping her?”

Sam gave him an irritated look. “I don’t like to think that I’m forcing myself on people, trying to cure them. Maybe Pris doesn’t need to be helped. From what I can tell, she doesn’t seem to have a problem that needs to be fixed. It sounds like she wants to take a step back from society.”

Chad looked startled at Sam’s cross tone. “Sorry, I didn’t mean to imply anything negative.”

She gave him a conciliatory smile. “I know that. Sorry I snapped. I didn’t sleep well last night, and it’s starting to be obvious.”

“You could take a nap,” suggested Chad. Then he smiled. “Never mind. I’ve never seen you take a nap the whole time I’ve known you.”

“I think they only succeed in messing me up for sleeping at night. No, I’ll just try to stay up until my normal bedtime.”

Sam’s phone rang, and Chad gave her a rueful look. “Here we go. I’m going out on a limb and saying that’s another neighbor taking you up on your offer to help.”

Sam looked at the number, which wasn't familiar to her. "Maybe I need to add the neighbors I've met as contacts on my phone, so I know which calls to avoid and which to answer."

She wished she'd already done that when she discovered Nora was on the other end. "Sam?" Nora asked in her reedy voice.

"Yes. Hi, Nora."

Chad grinned at Sam, and she rolled her eyes. Chad finished putting the groceries up and headed off to his man cave in the basement.

Nora said, "I'm a little worried about Julia Harper. You know her, don't you?"

"Yes, I've spoken with her a couple of times." She was the one who was in the disastrous park improvement project with George.

"Well, she's not answering her phone."

Sam smiled. She had the feeling that Julia might have been avoiding Nora for the very reasons that Sam was feeling like *she* should. "Maybe she has it on mute for a while, or she stepped away from it to do some housework or something."

"She didn't answer her door when I walked over there, though."

Sam was starting to suspect that Julia was doing an excellent job at evading Nora. Certainly better than Sam was doing. "Maybe she had earbuds in to listen to music while she cleaned. I do that a lot. It makes the time go faster."

Now Nora was getting irritated. "I don't think that's what's happened, Sam. I'm worried something has happened to her."

"Are you sure she's not running an errand? She might have accidentally left her phone at the house."

Nora said stiffly, "I don't think Julia would forget something like that. Are you going to help or not?"

Sam closed her eyes briefly, feeling a headache come on. "Of course I'll help. I'll meet you over at Julia's place in a few minutes." She hoped Julia, when she *did* answer the door, would forgive Sam for foisting Nora on her.

It already felt like the end of the day, but it was still just late-morning when Sam headed out. She drove this time because she hoped she could head right back home again after demonstrating to Nora that Julia was completely fine.

Nora was waiting impatiently for Sam when she parked the car in front of Julia's house. "Took you long enough," she growled.

Sam graciously ignored her. "All right, let's check on Julia."

First, she peeked into the garage, which had a couple of windows on the side. Julia's car was inside. "Looks like she's at home, unless she's gone for a walk around the neighborhood."

"She hasn't!" said Nora in a sour voice.

"Let's knock at the door," said Sam, determinedly cheerful.

Wanting the errand to be over, Sam knocked firmly on the door. Then she rang the doorbell twice for emphasis. No Julia. Sam wondered if she should have had Nora hide around the side of the house, in case Julia was avoiding the woman.

Nora sounded worried when she said, "Julia *always* answers her phone. She's very conscientious about it. She wouldn't want to worry me."

Sam said, "Okay. I'll do more checking." She turned the doorknob, and the door opened immediately. "Well, she hasn't locked up."

"That's *very* unlike her," said Nora.

Sam walked cautiously inside. "Julia? It's Sam."

"And Nora!" called Nora.

It was quiet inside.

Nora fidgeted. "Something's wrong."

Sam walked further inside. "Julia?"

Only silence greeted her. When she reached the living room, she saw Julia lying on the floor in a pool of blood, a decorative glass paperweight beside her.

Chapter Twelve

A minute later, after Sam had confirmed that Julia was indeed dead, Nora, and Sam were back outside, sitting in Sam's car. Nora was shivering, despite the warmth of the day. Noticing this, Sam hopped back out of the car and opened the trunk, finding her bag of emergency gear. She pulled out a soft blanket, unfurled it, and tucked it firmly around Nora before getting into the car.

Nora snuggled down into it, continuing to shiver. While they waited for the police to arrive, Sam ran her mouth, automatically giving boring details about her day, Arlo, and the process of moving. Her mouth was moving mindlessly while her brain was whirring. Even though the police had waffled at first on whether George Turner's death was murder, there was no doubt about Julia's. She'd been struck down with that paperweight. Had she known something about George's death? Had she figured something out? Had she represented a danger to the murderer?

It felt to Sam like she'd been inanely chatting for thirty minutes before the police cars sped up. In reality, though, it had been fewer than ten. Nora had finally stopped shivering and was looking steely-eyed and determined, a look Sam was sure boded ill for any killer she might happen across.

Sam and Nora quickly explained to the police what they'd seen. They watched as the officers walked cautiously inside before coming back out looking grim as they strung up police tape.

Then more police showed up. "The state police are here, too," noted Sam, looking at the cars.

Nora was less interested in the police representation. "What do you think happened?" she barked at Sam.

"Well, I think maybe Julia knew something. She knew enough to worry George's murderer, and they decided they needed to eliminate her so she wouldn't turn them over to the police," said Sam slowly.

"Eliminate her," said Nora caustically. "A sterile way of saying they hit her with a paperweight. I know about that thing, too. When I was at Julia's house one time, she showed it to me. She made it during a vacation to Sante Fe. It was at some sort of glassblowing class she attended there." A tear slipped out of Nora's eye, and she furiously wiped it away.

"I'm sorry," said Sam. "You and Julia were friends, weren't you?"

"We were," said Nora with a note of surprise in her voice. "I guess we were. I didn't really think of us that way. Now it's too late. Why didn't she go to the police if she knew something? Why did she let on to the killer that she knew he'd done it?"

Sam was asking herself the same questions. Could Julia have been blackmailing the murderer? It didn't seem likely, based on the fact she'd seemed financially secure. But George Turner had been financially secure too, and he had tried blackmailing Pris.

Sam said, "Maybe Julia wasn't absolutely sure what she'd seen. She was suspicious, but she wanted to make sure before she made any accusations."

Nora gave a satisfied bob of her head. "Yes. Yes, that sounds like Julia."

Sam continued, "She spoke to the murderer, just asking if there was an innocent explanation."

"A foolish thing to do," said Nora, an angry tone in her voice.

"Yes, but she wouldn't have wanted to ruin someone's life if there was nothing in what she'd seen. She was doing her due diligence."

"Which ended up killing her," said Nora.

They watched as the police consulted with each other. The detective who'd seemed in charge at the picnic was on the phone, perhaps calling for forensics help. Warren Watson, she thought his name was.

There was a tap on the window and Julia put it down for the detective. "Would you like us to step out of the car?" she asked.

The man considered this, then saw Nora, still shivering in the blanket. "It's all right. We can do this with both of you seated. I'm Detective Warren Watson, and I need some background on what happened today." He started off getting their names and addresses. Then he said, "First off, whose idea was it to visit Julia Harper today?"

"Mine," said Nora with a sniff. "I called her and she didn't answer. She didn't return my messages, which was very unusual."

"When did you start calling her?" asked the detective, making notes in a small notebook.

"It would have been last night."

He tapped his pencil against the paper. "What was so important that you needed to speak with her?"

Nora looked suddenly apprehensive. "That was something private between the two of us."

Sam had the feeling that Nora's claims of privacy would not fly with the detective. Not during a murder investigation.

He cocked his eyebrow and gave Nora a serious look. "There isn't any privacy when it comes to murder. I'd like to know why you were calling Julia. Why you were so determined to get in touch with her."

Nora gave an annoyed sigh. "All right. It's just that I wanted her opinion on something. I heard that Marcus Turner, George's son, was going to have a memorial service for his father. Julia and I weren't George's biggest fans, as I believe you're aware. I wanted to find out if Julia was going to go to the service or not."

His eyebrow quirked again. "That was the important thing?"

She glared at him. "It was to me. I didn't want to seem like a hypocrite, acting as if I were going to grieve at George's service. But I wasn't sure if it would make me appear hateful if I didn't go. I wanted Julia to help me decide."

He nodded. "And she didn't call you back. Was this surprising to you?"

Sam hid a smile. He was obviously thinking along the same wavelength that she'd done. Maybe Julia had avoided her phone calls.

"Of course it was surprising to me," snarled Nora, her white hair seemingly quivering with indignation. "Julia usually picked her phone up right away. If I ever had to leave a message, she'd call me back immediately. It was most out of character for her."

"So you continued calling her?"

"Not in an annoying way," said Nora, now sounding defensive. "I was simply concerned. I wondered if maybe her ringer was turned off last night. This morning, I resumed trying to get in touch with her again."

The police officer studied Nora thoughtfully through the car window. "You wouldn't have been trying to call her to keep her quiet, would you?"

Nora turned pale. "Whatever do you mean?"

"I mean, could Julia have figured out that you put the almonds in George Turner's salad? Did she see you sneaking around at the picnic and alert you she'd seen you? Is that why you were trying to get in touch with her? And, when she didn't answer the phone, did you come by the house and ensure she was quiet for good?"

Nora's mouth dropped open, and she quickly snapped it shut. "Of course not!"

"But you did come over here."

"Yes, but with Samantha . . . with Sam here." Nora gestured wildly at Sam.

Detective Watson glanced at Sam. "Because you wanted a witness when you 'discovered' the body?" His voice was coolly unflappable.

"No!"

"Where were you last night?" he asked.

Nora asked, "Is that when Julia died? Last night?"

"We're in the process of determining that," he said in that same cool tone. "Just give me a rundown of where you were since yesterday afternoon."

"Well, I was at home with Precious."

"Precious?" Watson quirked his eyebrow again.

"Yes, my dog. I was there from three in the afternoon until I came over here with Sam."

"Can anyone confirm that?" asked Watson. "Since Precious can't?"

Nora shook her head.

He said calmly, "How about recounting your movements?"

Nora blinked at him. "From yesterday and this morning?"

"Starting at three p.m."

Nora's eyes took on a faraway look as she mentally tried to travel back in time. "Right. At three, I was coming back in from taking Precious on a walk. We try to walk twice a day, unless the weather is bad or my hip is acting up."

Watson jotted down a note or two. Sam guessed that Nora's hip wasn't making the cut into his note-taking.

"Then I would have put the poop bags into the special can I have in the garage. It has one of those diaper pan deodorizers, which is nice."

This information also didn't make it into the notebook.

"Precious gets three snacks right after that. He'd started putting on weight, so the vet made me switch to training treats, which are a lot smaller than the big ones I'd been giving him. I think he notices and is upset about the change, but I figured his health was more important than his feelings. I do tell him he's a good boy, so he doesn't think he's being punished."

The notebook is no longer being held at attention, ready to hold all sorts of important statements from Nora.

Nora proceeded to cover the soap opera she watched (it had been recorded), the tomato soup and grilled cheese sandwich she'd prepared for her supper, the fruitless continued phone calls she'd made to Julia, the game show she'd watched with Precious after consuming her supper, and the early night she'd had after falling asleep reading a book that was very lulling.

After describing her two visits in the night to use the restroom, Watson held up his hand. "Is there any other *pertinent* information that you can give me? Did you leave the house again, for instance?"

"Of *course* I did. Precious would have exploded if I hadn't taken him out until now. We went on a morning walk. And I'd realized last night when I made my grilled cheese that I was using up the rest of the white American, so I went to the store this morning around nine."

Watson said, "Do you have the receipt from that trip? Or can you name the cashier who checked out your groceries for you?"

"I keep *all* of my receipts, young man. I advise you to do the same. Sometimes, despite my best efforts, I might get a container of blackberries that has moldy fruit near the bottom. I'll go back to the store, receipt in hand, and they'll allow me to get another container. Some people are so wasteful of their money. They'll just throw the rotten fruit away. But I think the grocery store has the responsibility to provide me with berries that don't go rotten in less than twenty-four hours."

Watson was looking very tired. "Got it. I'd like to ask you again about your relationship with George Turner."

Nora gave him a sour look. "The way you phrased that makes it sound as if George and I were romantically involved. Nothing could be further from the truth."

"What I'd particularly like to inquire about are the ways the issues between you escalated recently."

Nora said, "Escalated? What do you mean? The situation between George and me was precisely the same as it had been months before. Unfriendly but static."

"That's not exactly true though, is it?" asked Watson, leaning on the side of the car and fixing her with his serious expression. "The police had to become involved in the most recent events."

Nora gave Watson a horrified look. She said in a hoarse whisper, as if Sam couldn't hear her, "Not now! Not in front of the new neighbor."

"I won't say a word about it," said Sam.

Nora gave her a measuring look before finally deciding to trust her. "I suppose your imagination will fill in the blanks and make it something much worse than it was if I don't fill you in at this point. It was really nothing. Nothing at all."

"Nothing but mailbox vandalism and noise complaints," said Watson succinctly.

Nora colored a little. "The police were never able to prove that George's mailbox had anything at all to do with me. Besides, George was always the instigator in every instance of issues between us."

Watson raised his eyebrow. "You're saying he vandalized his own mailbox?"

"I'm saying nothing of the sort! I'm saying *I* didn't do it. Destruction of mailboxes is a federal offense. If I *had* done it, it would simply have been a way to indicate to George that I was unhappy with him."

Watson said, "Because of the noise issue."

"Well, he was certainly making lots of noise, officer. He was doing some sort of renovation and being as loud as he could. There was hammering at six in the morning! Hammering at ten at night! Naturally, I called the police to report him. There is a noise ordinance in Sunset Ridge, and George Turner obviously violated it. I believed it was my civic duty to turn him in."

"You might say, then, as I did, that the issues between the two of you escalated recently," said Watson complacently, having proved his point. Then he leaned forward, almost sticking his head inside Sam's vehicle. "I'm not saying that you intended on murdering George. But everyone knew he had an allergy to almonds. Maybe you had a bag of nuts in your kitchen, and you thought it would give him the signal that he needed to back off. Maybe you thought you were teaching him a lesson. That he would feel sick, but that would be all."

"I didn't! Look, I'm not saying there weren't hard feelings between George and me. But they weren't murderous feelings, not on his end and not on mine. I'm a member of the garden club, for heaven's sake. I go to the lunch club. I'm an upstanding citizen."

Sam would describe Nora as a very *excitable* citizen.

Watson changed tack and returned to a previous point. "But Julia saw you slip something in George's food at the picnic, didn't she? Maybe she didn't even realize what she saw at first. But the more Julia thought about it, the more she worried. It makes sense that you wanted to reach out to her. And it makes sense that Julia was trying to avoid you."

"You've got it all wrong," muttered Nora.

"Then straighten me out. Because I don't believe the story that you were trying to call Julia that many times because you wanted to know if she was going to a memorial service."

Watson waited patiently. Finally, Nora took a deep breath. "Okay. You're right. Sort of. That wasn't the *only* reason I was calling Julia. The main reason is that I thought maybe Julia had killed George."

Sam's eyes widened.

"What made you think that?" asked Watson.

"Well, mostly because of Julia's behavior at the picnic. It was different from usual. Ordinarily, Julia is very social. She's kind of one of those networking people, you know? She was very good at that. But at the picnic, I kept seeing her staring at George with this really focused expression on her face."

"Focused?"

Nora said impatiently, "Her eyes were fixed on him, officer. I thought it was odd at the time because Julia wants nothing more than to stay out of George's way. But there she was, not really visiting with people and staring at him."

Watson said, "And later on, you wondered if she might have been waiting for him to show some sort of reaction to the almonds."

"That's exactly right." Nora sounded relieved that Watson finally seemed to understand her. "I knew Julia had as many issues with George as I did. The more I thought about it, the more convinced I was that Julia must have tampered with George's food."

"But you didn't see her do it?"

Nora looked exasperated. "If I had, I'd have told you. My thought was that I was simply going to call Julia and tell her to turn herself in. That things would be much easier for her if she did. I guess part of me also wanted to hear that she'd been staring at George so fixedly because he had a stain on his shirt or something. I wanted her to tell me she was innocent." Then she lifted her chin defiantly. "But I also wanted to know if she would be at the memorial service. That was *not* a lie."

"Wouldn't she have been locked up for murder by then?" asked Watson mildly. "If you'd told her to turn herself in?"

"Well, I figured if she wasn't guilty, maybe she'd be going to the service. Anyway, clearly, I was completely wrong about everything. Poor Julia knew something and someone shut her up."

Watson nodded. "All right. You'd thought Julia did it. Now that Julia's not a likely option, who do you suspect now?"

Nora pursed her lips in displeasure. "I don't really like this process. It seems very uncivilized for me to comment on something that I know very little about."

Sam remembered that last time she thought Olivia had possibly been involved because of her affair with George. But she also knew that Nora was fond of Olivia and probably wouldn't want to implicate her. Nora gave Sam a stern look, as if to remind her she'd promised not to say anything about Olivia's involvement with George.

"I don't really have the slightest idea who did it, since Julia didn't. But if I were the police, I'd be speaking with Marcus Turner. It seems as if he might have the strongest motive. He's surely going to be inheriting money from his father's estate, and he and his dad didn't have the strongest relationship. George was a rather nasty man and perhaps the apple didn't fall far from the tree."

"Got it," said Watson, making another quick note in his notebook. Then he turned and gave Sam a small smile. "You've had a pretty harrowing introduction to the neighborhood."

Sam thought that was an interesting adjective for a detective to use. She said cautiously, "Oh, well, it hasn't been *that* bad. It's just been a little surprising." She had the feeling, though, that Chad was going to be very alarmed at a second dead body in Maple Hills in the space of a week.

"So Nora called you up this morning. Was that unexpected?"

Nora gave her a concerned look.

Sam said, "Nora is a friendly woman. I wasn't too surprised, no. I'm also currently making a concerted effort in the subdivision to get to know my new neighbors and help them out when I can."

"That seems unusually generous." Watson's eyes narrowed as if generosity was rather suspicious to him.

Nora broke in. "Sam's running for the open HOA president spot."

Warren Watson gave her a thoughtful look.

"But don't be thinking that she knocked off the old HOA president just to satisfy her political aspirations," said Nora with a cackle.

Sam gave a tight smile.

Nora added, "Seriously, though, she didn't even have the chance to meet George before he died. They were late for the picnic."

Watson nodded. "What about Julia Harper? Had you met her?"

Sam cleared her throat and sat up straight in the driver's seat, as if good posture would make her seem even more trustworthy than she already was. "Yes, I had met her, actually. I spoke to her the afternoon of George's death. I went out for a walk, and she was outside doing yardwork. She seemed to be clearing her head."

Watson cocked an eyebrow again. "What gave you that impression?"

"Oh, just that she appeared to have something on her mind. She was anxious about something. Julia was attacking her yard with gusto, that's for sure."

Watson jotted down a couple of notes. "Did she share with you what she was anxious about?"

"No. But then, I'd just met her, so I hardly expected any confidences. I was also in contact with her later because she emailed me some of the HOA information—the bylaws and the resident directory."

Watson said, "Which would be useful for your run for office, presumably."

"That's right."

"But you have no idea who might have wanted to murder Julia? Did she mention she was having trouble with any person in the neighborhood?" asked Watson.

Sam noticed Nora tense beside her at the question. But when she turned to look at her, she was relaxed again.

"Mainly, she spoke about her issues with George Turner. She also mentioned that the vice president of the HOA could be difficult to deal with, too," said Sam.

"The person you're presumably running against."

"Yes, Hank. Presumably. The ballots haven't been finalized yet."

Watson nodded. "Okay. Let me get your information again, so I'll have it handy. Then you're welcome to head on your way."

It sounded less like an invitation and more like an order. But Sam realized over the past few minutes that neighbors were spilling into their yards, looking curiously over at Sam and Nora. She was sure the police wanted everyone to clear out and stay out of their way.

As Watson walked away, Sam said to Nora, "Do you want me to drop you by your house?"

But Nora had apparently also noticed the concerned neighbors grouping around. She shook her head. "It's only down the street. The walk will do me good."

Being the center of attention as the person who knew what was going on, would also likely do her some good, thought Sam.

Nora said, "I'm sorry about getting you involved in this whole mess. I had no idea we'd find Julia murdered in there. You know that."

It sounded more like a question. "Of course I do," said Sam, although she knew nothing of the sort.

"I thought maybe she was ill and needed medical attention. That she'd had a heart attack or something." Nora shook her head, looking genuinely sad. "I'm sorry she's gone. I enjoyed talking with her."

"Call me if there's anything you need, Nora. And please take care." Sam didn't have to say more. Nora was well aware there was a murderer in Maple Hills.

Chapter Thirteen

Sam barely even noticed anything on the drive home. It was almost as if she were on autopilot. She walked in the house, stooping absentmindedly to rub Arlo, who greeted her with an energetic wag of his little tail. "Hey baby," she murmured, leaning her face into his fur.

Chad came up from the basement, chatting about a baseball game he'd watched and some incredible play he'd witnessed. Several sentences in, he noticed Sam didn't seem to be paying much attention. "Is everything okay?" he asked.

"Not really," admitted Sam. "Nora and I did a wellness check on Julia and found her dead. Murdered."

"What?"

"Murdered. With a glass paperweight. It was pretty awful."

Chad hurried over to put his arms around her. "I'm so sorry. Are you okay? What happened?"

"Well, Nora was the person who called me right before I left the house. She was worried because she'd tried calling Julia for a while and hadn't gotten an answer or a return of her messages."

Chad said, "And she wanted you to go check on her with her. Because you'd offered to be so helpful."

Sam ignored his pointed tone. Sometimes it seemed like Chad could be envious of all the other people who took up her time. "That's right. I figured at first that Julia was probably trying to avoid Nora because Nora's so nosy and gets into everyone's business. But when she didn't answer the door, and her car was there, I started wondering if something had happened to her, too. So I walked in her door."

"It was unlocked?"

Sam nodded. "And there she was. So I called the police, of course, and tried to make Nora feel better. Nora had considered the two of them friends. Then we both had to speak to the police. It was that same detective that was at the picnic. Warren Watson."

"Did he give any kind of indication of what he thought might have happened?" Chad frowned.

"No, that's not the kind of thing they like to disclose, I guess. He was more interested in asking Nora and me questions. Especially Nora."

Chad raised his eyebrows. "But Nora is a little old lady. You're saying Watson thought Nora might have killed George and Julia?"

"Well, he definitely seemed to imply that he could see Nora having slipped George the almonds. It sounded, from what he was saying, that their issues had really escalated recently. There was something about mailbox vandalism and noise complaints."

"Okay. Still, it sounds like two neighbors behaving badly. It's very hard for me to picture Nora as some sort of serial killer." Chad reached out to Arlo and the dog deftly moved behind Sam's legs out of reach. Chad sighed.

Sam rubbed the dog absently. "Right. I mean, I can get what you're saying. I don't think I would underestimate Nora, though. Not in any way."

Chad leaned back in his chair, flinging his feet up on the ottoman. "My problem is that I'm getting pretty worried about this neighborhood."

"Maple Hills? I don't think we can lump the whole subdivision in with what happened with George and Julia. Those were isolated incidents."

"Were they?" asked Chad. "Because it seems like we've picked the wrong neighborhood to me. It *seemed* like a sleepy little hamlet. But in reality, there's a murderer afoot."

Sam decided to change the subject. Having just unpacked the house, the last thing she wanted to contemplate was another move. Besides, she liked what she'd seen so far of Maple Hills. Aside from the murders, naturally. The neighbors were friendly, the yards well-kept, and there were fun ways to connect with others in the neighborhood. "Anything happen while I was gone?"

"You mean besides a murder?" asked Chad darkly.

"Yes, besides that."

"Actually, someone did call the house phone. I guess you must have put the number on your signs. They said they tried to reach your cell, but you didn't pick up," said Chad.

"Oops," said Sam, reaching into her pocket for her phone. "I turned it off after I called the police because I didn't want any interruptions." She turned the phone back on. "Yeah, I see I've got a missed call."

"It was a woman asking if she could run by this evening for one of your campaign signs. She wanted to put it in her yard."

Sam beamed. "Well, that's nice. Who was it?"

"She said she was the mom of the boy you took to school today." Chad raised an eyebrow. "You're really going out on a limb for this election. You should parlay your popularity into a bigger office. Governor, or something."

Sam snorted. "Not exactly something that sounds like fun to me."

"But being president of the HOA does?" Chad sounded very doubtful at that prospect.

"Sure. Fun because the residents have such low expectations, and I might really make some improvements. Make a difference. The higher up you go in politics, the less control you have."

"Strange but true," said Chad. Then he gave her a fetching look. "On a completely different subject, could you use your tech prowess to help me out with my phone? The thing crashes all the time. I was thinking about getting a new one, then I realized I live with someone who can fix the problem." He gave Sam a winning grin. "It's nice being married to a tech guru."

"Sure, hand it over," said Sam. "As long as I can count on your vote," she added in a stern voice.

Chad gave her a kiss. Then he said, "Do you miss it? The tech world, I mean?"

"Not a bit."

The HOA secretary sent out an email later that afternoon to let everyone in Maple Hills know of George Turner's memorial service at the Methodist church the next day. "We should probably go," said Sam.

Chad seemed more resistant about going to the service of someone he'd met only briefly. "Really? It's not as if anyone would think twice if we didn't go. You didn't even have the chance to meet the man."

"It'll give us the opportunity to spend time with other neighbors."

Chad had sighed. "What time is it tomorrow?"

"Noon."

So they made plans to attend. But when it was time to leave, Chad was suddenly stricken with a migraine. He took to his bed with one of the gel masks he kept in the freezer. Sam headed out the door.

When Sam walked into the Methodist church, her first impression was that someone had spared no expense for a big send-off for George. But in the pew reserved for family, there was only Marcus. As she sat down farther back in the church, she wondered why Marcus had found it necessary to spend so much money. Maybe he was trying to show everyone, including the police officers discreetly sitting in the back, that he was a grieving son, not a killer.

The church was adorned with lush magnolia and gardenia arrangements, making the whole sanctuary smell like spring. There was a full choir in attendance, as well as a chamber music orchestra. The service had readings, eulogies, hymns, a meditation, and what can only be called full performances from the choir and orchestra. It was quite a production and something Sam had never seen at a service.

The reception was held in the church's dining room. There was what looked to be a comfort food buffet, and again there had been no cost spared. It was more customary in the South for there to be casseroles from a church committee that handled funerals, with food doled out by church ladies. This one was definitely catered, most likely by one of the fancier establishments in Sunset Ridge's charming downtown. Serving tables were laden with Southern comfort food, including shrimp and grits, fried chicken, collard greens, and cornbread.

Samantha was served a little bit of everything, then found a spot to sit. Even the tables were adorned with magnolia centerpieces of magnolia branches and candles.

Marcus was walking around the room, speaking to different people. His handsome face was strained, but smiling. The police were still hanging around on the outskirts of the room, watching everyone with interest.

This made Sam watch everyone, too. At the funeral, the mourners had appeared to be dry-eyed, and that was the case here, too. Various people hugged Marcus, and some seemed to share light-hearted stories, perhaps of George, with him. They'd laugh and hug again.

After a few minutes, Marcus spotted Sam and made his way over to her table. She put down her fork and started to stand, but he motioned her to sit down and joined her.

Sam said politely, "It was a lovely service. And the reception is wonderful, too. A nice way to recognize your father."

Marcus's gaze flitted back over to the police officers, who appeared to be keeping an eye on him. "I'm glad you think so. I appreciate you coming."

Suddenly, Sam felt an arm go around her. She whirled around, relaxing when she saw Chad. "Headache better?"

He nodded. "Once I woke up from that nap, I felt a lot better. I thought I'd join you." He extended his other arm toward Marcus. "I'm Chad Prescott."

"Marcus Turner. Good to meet you."

"Actually, I believe we met at the picnic, just briefly," said Chad. "I'm so sorry about your father. I met him at the picnic, and he seemed like a great guy."

"Thanks," said Marcus, a little stiffly.

Sam suspected her ability to speak to Marcus was about to get stifled. She did want to ask him about Julia's death. She said to Chad, "Why don't you grab yourself something to eat? The food is fantastic, and it might help keep your headache at bay."

Chad looked chipper at this. "That's true. It smells amazing."

As he walked away, Sam said, "Have the police made any progress on your dad's case?"

Marcus cast an irritated gaze toward the police again. "No. They've been in contact with me, but not because of any breakthroughs. They wanted to hear about my whereabouts regarding Julia Harper's death." He sighed. "That was a shocker."

"It was, wasn't it?"

Marcus said, "I was back at Dad's house, finishing clearing out when Nora told me you and she had been the ones to find Julia. That must have been terrible for you."

"It was especially bad for Nora. She'd been so determined to find her, believing that she needed help of some kind. I don't think she really imagined that Julia could be dead."

Marcus gave a short laugh. "*I* couldn't really imagine that she could be dead. I mean, what's going on in Maple Hills? From what the police were saying, it sounded like maybe Julia knew something about Dad's murder."

"Did the police give you a hard time about Julia?"

Marcus said, "Sure they did. But I'd never even spoken two words to the woman. All I'd done was listen to Dad rant about her. Why would I murder someone I'd never even met?"

Sam nodded, keeping quiet. She'd found silence could be an excellent device. Sometimes it prompted people to talk more, to fill in the gap in conversation.

It seemed to work in this instance. Marcus said, "The police were also harassing me about somebody else. Dad's new relationship. They think I was worried Dad was going to change his will, cutting me out in favor of his new girlfriend." His tone was bitter. "I'm not saying I didn't have serious concerns about her. I wasn't sure about her intentions. And I wasn't sure she was going to be a positive influence over Dad. But seriously? Killing Dad to keep him from changing his will? That's like something out of a bad movie."

Sam said carefully, "I'd think the police would think it seemed less likely because you have a successful career of your own."

Marcus hesitated before saying slowly, "Yeah. The only problem is that I'm saddled with a bunch of debt. The police made a lot out of that. But I'm not the only person to have tons of school debt. I've got loans to pay back for both college and medical school. It'll take forever to be debt-free. But I'd never have thought of killing my father as a way out of debt."

"Did the police focus on any suspects in particular?"

Marcus gave her a wry smile. "Besides me, you mean? Not really. Of course, I've been thinking about it. Clearly, I was wrong when I thought Julia might have murdered Dad. That seems totally impossible now that she's been murdered. Since the police seem to want to pin things on me, I've been spending lots of time mulling everything over. I know this is going to sound crazy, but now I'm wondering if Nora could be involved."

"What makes you think that?" asked Sam.

"I don't know. She lived right next door to Dad, and the two of them couldn't stand each other. I wouldn't have been at all surprised if *Nora* had been the victim instead of my dad. I'd have known for sure who was guilty then." His mouth twisted in a smile. "Plus, I saw Nora right up in Dad's face at the picnic. She definitely had the opportunity. Maybe Julia saw her put the almonds in his salad, and Nora had to kill her, too."

He rubbed his temples as if a headache was coming on. "I don't know. Don't listen to me. I feel like I'm grasping at straws. The fact of the matter is, I loved Dad, but I know he was a difficult person. He and I had differences of opinion, and he had them with plenty of other people, too. I don't think I should be the only suspect here." He glanced up and his mouth twisted again. "Looks like Chad is coming back. I should speak with some other people. Thanks again for coming."

Chad carefully set down a paper plate that was groaning with fried chicken, mac, and cheese casserole, and ham biscuits. He said sadly, "I couldn't resist this stuff. I'm probably going to be in a food coma after eating all this. If I don't have another calorie this week, it'll be too soon."

"How's your headache doing?" asked Sam.

"It's gone, except for the fact that the muscles in my head are hurting. Sort of sad that the muscles get all cramped up during those headaches." He took a bite of his chicken and closed his eyes. "Oh my gosh, this is good." He sat, eating happily for a few moments, then quirked an eyebrow at Sam. "What was on Marcus's mind?"

"He's worried that the police are considering him the primary suspect."

Chad nodded. "That makes sense. I mean, it makes sense that they suspect him and it makes sense that Marcus is worried about it. After all, he's probably got the most to gain from his father's death."

"Maybe," said Sam.

"Don't look now, but I think we're about to get a visitor."

Sam, of course, couldn't help but look. She saw Nora walking toward them and groaned before carefully giving a welcoming smile.

"Make sure she doesn't stick anything in our food," murmured Chad before the old woman plonked herself down in an empty seat next to Sam.

"Quite the extravaganza, don't you think?" asked Nora.

"The memorial service, you mean?" Sam knew quite well what Nora was referring to, but thought she should point out that it was a funeral.

"If you want to call it that," said Nora with a sniff. "I think it was designed to make Marcus look good." She narrowed her eyes at Sam. "I saw you speaking with Marcus for quite a while. What was he saying?"

Chad looked curious, too.

"We were talking about his father's death. And Julia's, too."

Nora asked, "What did he have to say about Julia's?"

"Well, not a whole lot, considering he'd never met her. He said his entire opinion of Julia was formed by his dad's rants, so he was pretty biased."

Nora leaned forward, her chest perilously close to being covered by her shrimp and grits. "What did you say?"

"Marcus hadn't met Julia," repeated Sam, this time louder in case Nora was hard of hearing. Although she hadn't gotten the impression that she was.

Nora leaned back in her chair again, a satisfied expression on her face. "That's what I thought you said. And that is, categorically, a lie. From my backyard perch, I've seen Julia, George, and Marcus arguing with each other in George's yard. It sounds like Marcus wants to cover his tracks."

When Nora's conversation turned to more desultory topics involving grudges against various neighbors for a compendium of perceived offenses, Sam, and Chad made a speedy exit. Chad was in his own car, of course, having arrived later. "Heading back home?" asked Chad before he climbed into his vehicle.

"Oh, probably. I should let Arlo out and maybe take him on a walk. It's a nice day, after all. Do you think you could run an errand for me?"

Chad gave her a salute with a cheery grin. "At your service, ma'am."

"Could you pick up the prescriptions we have at the drugstore? I think you and I both have items that are ready."

"Gotcha. I might run by the grocery store too, while I'm out. Maybe I can whip us up a meal. One of my specialty breakfasts or something."

Sam gave him a smile, although she was biting back a sigh. She never could quite grasp Chad's grocery shopping approach. Her own involved a digital store flyer, digital coupons, a list that was organized by aisle, and a meal plan. Chad's seemed to consist of walking randomly through the store and picking up items that appealed to him. "Sounds good," she said in what she hoped was a supportive tone.

Back at home, Arlo was indeed ready to walk. As they set out, Arlo had an extra spring in his step. It was quiet in the neighborhood, with some neighbors lingering at the service and others at work. A retired man doing yardwork loved on Arlo for a few minutes, which the small dog ate up happily. Sam looked at Aiden, the former cop's, house to see if he was home. She'd like to ask more questions about Julia's death and wondered if he'd spoken to his contact with the police. But his car wasn't there. She remembered it was a Thursday, and he should be teaching.

She found herself pulled inextricably toward Pris Lawrence's house. Sam knew she should probably wait for the woman to reach out again. But she'd seemed so anxious the last time she'd seen her. She hoped that, even though it wasn't trash collection day, she might get a chance meeting with her when she walked by. Maybe Pris would drive in or out of her house. She'd hadn't been at George's memorial service, but then Sam certainly hadn't expected her to be there.

But when Sam approached her house, she heard a deep voice speaking to a quiet, female one at the end of the long driveway. She couldn't see who the man was because Pris's yard was too wooded, and the leaves hadn't yet started to fall.

"She's with that man again," said a grouchy voice behind her.

Chapter Fourteen

Sam whirled around, as did Arlo.

"Sorry to startle you," said an elderly man, holding the leash of his own small dog. "I just saw you looking down at Pris Lawrence's house."

"You say she's with a man?" asked Sam, although she'd heard the deep timbre, herself.

The man nodded. He had a grizzled head of hair and wore a long-sleeved shirt and khakis, despite the warmth of the day. "He's been down visiting there before. He's not good for her."

"Not good for her? What do you mean? You think he's abusive?" asked Sam.

The man shook his head impatiently. "I don't know, do I? I don't ever see Pris, not unless she wants to be seen. Which she doesn't. I've seen her sneak out to get her mail after dark, even though she's at home all day long."

"I'm Samantha Prescott, by the way."

"John Parsons," he said. "You're running for HOA president, aren't you? I've seen the signs."

"That's right. But I'm really wanting everyone in the neighborhood to feel like they can come to me for help. I want residents to feel it's *their* HOA. That's one reason I'm worried about Pris." It wasn't much of a segue, but Sam wanted to switch the conversation back to Pris, since he might offer some perspective. "I was hoping she was simply shy. She did say something about having moved from a dysfunctional neighborhood. Pris might simply want to stay out of Maple Hills drama."

John snorted. "Well, she's creating drama of her own, by being a hermit."

"So you're wondering if she's in a bad relationship? You think maybe that's adding to the issues she's already having?"

John looked as if he was going to use his "don't know!" statement again, but then stopped. "Maybe. All I know is that there used to be a man coming down to see her last summer. Then he stopped for a while. Now he's back again, and she won't let him inside. So there are some loud voices going on outside Pris's house. One time, I thought about going down there and getting involved. Throwing the guy off the property, if that's what it took."

"You decided not to?"

John nodded. "Yeah. I started thinking about how the cops always hate to go to domestic disturbances. You never really know what you're stepping into, do you? And I'm not a young guy anymore."

His small dog gingerly approached Arlo to sniff him. Sam watched carefully to see Arlo's reaction and whether he felt uncomfortable at all. Arlo looked a little startled, but then wagged his tail.

John grunted. "Looks like those two have made friends. Peanut rarely does that." He paused. "Wait, isn't that the yappy dog that used to live down the street?" He gave Sam a look of respect. "Well, now. You really *are* trying to fix things, aren't you?"

"If I can. And Arlo is a sweetheart. He really doesn't bark at all now that he's living inside as a member of the family." Arlo wagged his tail again at this.

John said, "You've had a trial by fire, being new to the neighborhood. Two murders in the last week." He shook his head. "I promise it's not usually like that here. It's one of the safest neighborhoods in Sunset Ridge. I've been here for decades and nothing like that has happened."

Sam said, "What's your perspective on it? Since you've been such a long-time resident."

"On the murders? I figured Julia had done George in, of course. Those two fought like cats and dogs. Now I'm thinking Nora is behind it all."

Sam kept finding herself surprised when people mentioned Nora as a suspect. Was this intrinsic ageism that she wasn't aware she had? Nora certainly wasn't someone to be underestimated. "Really?" she asked.

"Don't look so surprised. That woman is mean as a snake. At least, she can be when she doesn't get her way. And George was making sure she was getting her way as little as possible. I was walking Peanut when I heard the two of them practically coming to blows in George's front yard. They didn't seem to care a bit that they had an audience."

"What was the argument about?"

John said, "Oh, some nonsense about George's grass being too high and his bushes being untrimmed. And George was giving it right back to Nora regarding the loud music she was playing."

"Loud music?"

"Yeah, apparently Nora found some heavy metal music online and was blasting it. She was wearing earplugs, so it didn't bother her. I bet it bothered Precious, though."

Sam said slowly, "Okay. Yeah, that sounds like quite an altercation."

John glanced around him as if someone might try to listen in. He said in a low voice, "That's not the only person who might have been out to get George. There's Olivia, too."

Sam carefully didn't let on that she knew anything about Olivia's affair with George. "Olivia Stanton?"

"That's right. She's married to that big-shot. Or the guy who thinks he's a big-shot, anyway. He's always trying to throw his weight around. But she was sneaking around seeing George." John added hastily, "Nobody knows about it, so keep it under your hat. The only reason I know is because I saw them together in town when I was taking Peanut to walk in the park. George was sitting in Olivia's car."

Sam said, "But why would Olivia want to murder George if she was having an affair with him?"

"Because, knowing George, he wasn't being discreet about it. George was fond of bragging—how important he was at his old job, his volunteering accomplishments, his surgeon son. Having an affair with a pretty, younger woman was bound to come up." John looked at his watch. "Look, I'd better head on my way. Got to finish Peanut's walk before I go to the store." He paused for a second. "Reckon you've got my vote. Good to meet you."

Sam certainly didn't want to show up for a visit with Pris if she were in the middle of an argument. So she headed back home. "We'll try again tomorrow, Arlo," she said.

Arlo seemed to understand perfectly.

However, Pris wasn't out the next day. Nor the following. Sam harnessed her energy to focus on the impending election. Proxy ballots were distributed through email, a modern twist to the traditional voting process. The electronic buzz hummed with anticipation as homeowners clicked their preferences, submitting their votes with the tap of a button. The HOA meeting loomed on the horizon, and Sam, with her characteristic enthusiasm, embarked on a final push to secure support, making an effort to be very visible in the neighborhood.

Then the evening of the HOA meeting arrived—a gathering that rivaled Game of Thrones in intrigue. Sam arrived early, clutching her acceptance speech and concession speech notes like a lifeline. The community center buzzed with anticipation. Hank, the other candidate, had clearly attempted to dress up and adjusted his bowtie nervously. According to what Nora told Sam on the phone earlier that day, his tenure as vice president had been marked by indecisiveness and an inexplicable obsession with topiary sculptures, which he proposed for the front entrance. Astoundingly, he appeared to be wearing cufflinks. Hank's smug features and bowtie telegraphed an air of financial wizardry—the kind that whispered, "I've juggled stocks, bonds, and offshore accounts." Sam strongly suspected he'd once been a hedge fund manager.

The meeting began, starting with business that had already been started earlier in the year. Hank droned on about budget allocations, tree-trimming schedules, and the urgent matter of replacing the lights on the subdivision's sign. Sam's eyes glazed over. She had bigger fish to fry—like ensuring that the potholes didn't swallow small pets.

Then came the moment of truth. The votes were counted, and the room held its collective breath. Hank's mustache twitched. The HOA secretary cleared her throat.

"And the new HOA president is..." she paused for dramatic effect, "Sam!"

Applause erupted and some shutterbug neighbor was taking lots of photos with their flash on, blinding Sam. Still, Sam's heart soared. Hank's face turned a shade of crimson that clashed horribly with his bowtie. Sam stepped forward, accepting the ceremonial gavel. She vowed to fill the potholes, trim the hedges, and be an advocate for the residents any way she could. Sam spotted Nora across the room, looking smugly satisfied at Sam's win, as if she'd personally been responsible.

And so, in the twilight of that HOA meeting, Sam became more than just a woman in sensible flats—she became the keeper of lawns and defender of neighborhood roads.

"I guess I'm the first husband now," said Chad with a chuckle as he gave Sam a hug at the end of the meeting as they were walking back home. "You deserve the win. You put a ton of work into every part of the process."

"And now it's time to get the real work started," said Sam. "I think I'm going to kick things off with a movie night."

"That sounds like fun," said Chad. "A family-friendly night? Or more of an adult thing?"

"I think it would be better to start out with a family-friendly night, don't you? Just to get more people there. I can make a brief speech at the beginning, thanking everyone for their votes and throwing out ideas I have for Maple Hills." Sam was already mentally coming up with the text for her speech. Then she stopped. "For right now, though, I need to collect my campaign signs."

"I can do that for you."

Sam said, "Thanks, but I think I'll take care of it. I can use the opportunity to visit with neighbors."

Plus, it gave her another opportunity to scout out Pris's house after being thwarted the last couple of times she'd been by. This time, Arlo-free, she headed out in the car. After getting two of the signs, she drove up to Pris's house. She hesitated, then drove all the way down the long driveway to the house. Pris had dropped in on Sam, after all. Sam hoped she wouldn't have an issue with Sam dropping in. It was a Sunday, though. Because of her aversion to public places, though, she guessed Pris wouldn't be attending any services.

Sam tapped quietly on the door. Then, when there was no answer, she knocked a bit louder. Pris finally came to the door, looking tired and irritable. But when she saw Sam, she gave her a big smile. "I'm glad it's you," she said, opening the door. "The police have been by again, and I thought they'd come back."

"Is it okay if I come in?" asked Sam. "I wanted to check in on you."

Pris said, "How about if we sit on the back deck?"

Sam followed Pris around the back of the house where stairs led to a generous deck and a view of the dense woods surrounding the house.

Pris looked down at her hands. "I'm so exhausted, Sam. The police seem convinced I have something to do with Julia's death."

"I can't think why they would be. Did you even have any interactions with her?"

Pris shook her head. "No, I'd never met her. I'd seen her out in the neighborhood, but I never spoke to her. And the cops keep pressuring me for an alibi. But I live alone. I don't have any alibi for Tuesday night or Wednesday morning." She rubbed her face. "I know the police are doing their jobs. But defending myself repeatedly wears me out."

"I'm sorry you're having to go through this, Pris."

Pris sighed. "They've even been asking me if I had any knowledge of George's allergies." She gave a short laugh. "How would I? It's not as if George and I were friends who shared those kinds of details."

Sam nodded.

Pris said, "I don't even like almonds. I don't have them in my house. It's all such a mess. I wish I'd never gone to that picnic."

"I know you said you went out of a sense of obligation, right? You felt you needed to take part in a neighborhood event."

"That's right," said Pris. "Nora told me that people were talking about me. I thought if I made an appearance, maybe everyone would drop it."

"You know Nora?"

Pris made a face. "Nora has pushed her way into my business a couple of times. Shown up at my door, brought me food. She's a very persistent woman." She gave a small smile. "Nora was very nosy with asking how I could stay inside all day and afford to live. I explained the concept of remote work to her."

"What kind of work do you do?"

Pris said, "Banking. It's a great job for me because the office doesn't require me to go in except for once a year. It's not a short drive to Charlotte, so I'm very grateful they don't demand too much from me."

"That sounds like it works out perfectly."

Pris rubbed her head. "With the police over here all the time, I'm sure people in Maple Hills are talking. Now they probably don't just think I'm strange . . . they think I've killed two people. Just because I'm not as social as they want."

Sam said cautiously, "It's none of my business, and you definitely don't have to answer this question if you don't want to. But is everything okay? Are you safe?"

Pris seemed startled by the question. "Safe?"

Sam said, "I was walking Arlo recently and heard you arguing with a man. I was worried maybe you were in a dangerous situation."

Pris looked down. "No, it's not dangerous. He's got a temper, that's all. I'm all right, I promise."

"Okay." Sam gave her a steady look. "You'll let me know if that changes, though?"

"I will." Pris hesitated. "You get along with your husband well, don't you?"

"Chad? Yes, we get along well together."

"Maybe someday I'll find someone like him." Pris gave her a sad smile.

"I hope you do."

Pris said, "You haven't heard anything from the police, have you? About making progress on the case?"

Sam must have looked confused because Pris added, "It's just that you see so many more neighbors than I do. I wondered if maybe some of them had given you information."

"Not really. Did you have any ideas for anyone who might have killed George or Julia?" It seemed very unlikely, since Pris had taken every possible means to stay away from her neighbors.

"I've been really thinking about it," said Pris. "Trying to remember if I saw anything or heard anything at the picnic. The police asked me a lot of questions about Marcus, though. George's son, you know. They wanted to know if I'd met him, what my impressions were of him, and how often he was in Maple Hills. I wasn't able to help them out with that at all." She shrugged helplessly. "I know the police believe I'm trying to be evasive. But I just don't know anything."

"Hopefully, other neighbors will verify that you don't interact with the neighbors very much. I'll certainly tell the police that, if they ask me."

"Thanks," said Pris, giving her a small smile. Then she said, "Oh! I forgot to congratulate you. I saw the email saying you'd won the HOA president position."

"Thanks!" said Sam, beaming at her. "I'm planning to jump right in with making some changes around here. Let me know if there's anything you'd like me to work on. One of the first things I'm setting up is a movie night. It'll be family-friendly. You definitely don't need to come if it'll make you feel uncomfortable, but it might be one of the easier Maple Hills events to attend. There'll be less need for visiting with the neighbors."

"I'll think about it. Thanks, Sam."

"Of course! I'll email about it soon. I should probably run now, but thanks for the visit. And, like I said, call me anytime."

On the way home, Sam mulled everything over. Movie night, the murders, Arlo, the HOA. She felt like there were some bits and pieces that she still needed to make a full picture of what had happened. It was frustrating that what she knew wasn't quite complete enough to present the solution. When she drove past Aiden Wood's house, she slowed down. Sure enough, he was stepping out of his car. She pulled into his driveway and gave him a friendly wave. He put up his hand to shield his eyes from the sun, then smiled when he saw Sam.

"Everything okay?" he asked. He was carrying a couple of books, which he set down on the hood of his car.

"It's all good. Well, as good as it can be, I guess."

Aiden nodded. "I heard you were the one who found Julia."

"Yes, along with Nora."

Aiden leaned against his car. "Sorry you had to go through that." He paused. "You'd met Julia before?"

"She and I had visited a little while the afternoon after the picnic. I couldn't believe what had happened. Nora had been trying to reach her and started worrying, so she recruited me to go over."

Aiden nodded again. "I'm not surprised that Nora spearheaded the wellness visit."

"I was wondering if you'd heard anything about Julia's death. Since you still have contacts at the police department."

Aiden's eyes twinkled. "I see. You're wanting to pump me for information. But I did bring up the subject."

Sam had the grace to blush. "Sorry. I realize this is nosy of me."

Aiden said slowly, "As before, I'd like to make sure this information stays between you and me. But it sounds like they were able to collect some physical evidence at the scene."

"Like DNA? Footprints?"

Aiden said, "They weren't that specific. But the perpetrator left evidence behind . . . evidence that doesn't match anything in their database."

"So probably not a career criminal," said Sam.

Aiden shook his head. "Probably not a career criminal, anyway. Especially if it's someone who was at that picnic and is now trying to cover his tracks. At any rate, the evidence should help with a prosecution once it goes to trial."

"That's good news." Sam smiled at him. "Thanks for that. Enjoy your Sunday! Sorry I interrupted you."

He gave Sam a slow grin in return. "Any time."

Chapter Fifteen

When she got home, Chad greeted her. "Everything okay? Got all the signs?"

"Every one of them. I guess I'll put these downstairs in storage for the next election."

Chad snorted. "Probably not even necessary. Once everyone sees you run the HOA, they'll never want to have anyone else in the office."

"That's sweet of you to say, but you're likely biased." Sam opened up the fridge and pulled out the chicken for the enchiladas she was making for dinner.

"Did you come across anyone on the way?"

"Hmm?" asked Sam, looking at the recipe for the enchiladas on her phone.

"When you were out collecting the signs. Did you speak to more of your suspects?"

Sam said, "Not really. I spoke to that woman, Pris, again."

"Which one was she? Was she the one who had the kid who missed the school bus?"

Sam said, "That was a different one. This is the one who was on the fringe of the picnic. The one who came over to our house. You met her briefly."

"Oh, right. The recluse. How are you managing so many visits with her? Never mind. It's because you're you. Is she one of the suspects?"

"Well, the police seem to think she is. But unless she's very good at sleight of hand, I don't think she is. The only problem is that she had a pretty good motive for wanting George Turner dead."

Chad's voice sounded surprised. "She did? The recluse?"

"That's right. Apparently, George was trying to blackmail Pris. He knew she had a police record. It was a DWI, and Pris was worried he was going to tell the whole neighborhood about it."

Chad said, "That sounds like a pretty good motive. And you went over to visit with her? I'm getting worried about you, Sam. Knocking on doors made sense when you were campaigning, but it doesn't make sense now. Julia Harper was murdered for knowing too much. I don't want the same thing to happen to you."

"Point taken," said Sam, shredding a block of cheese. "Anyway, I don't think you have to worry about Pris."

"Yes, but what about Nora? It seems like you're spending a ton of time with her."

Sam said, "I wouldn't say *that*. She's simply unavoidable sometimes."

"Discovering murder victims with her," continued Chad in a disapproving and still worried tone.

"Well, I don't plan on doing that again, at least not anytime soon. Seriously, don't worry. I'm about to devote most of my time to reworking the HOA. I want to review the bylaws, change the way we handle architectural reviews, and more." Sam reached for her planner. "Which reminds me I wanted to go through the past HOA emails and see what I can glean from them."

But Chad appeared to still be stuck on Nora. "I've been meaning to tell you I remembered something from the picnic."

Sam turned her head. "Really? Something about George's death?"

"Not really. Or maybe. It's hard to say. It was just something that happened before he started having his reaction. It was Nora. She came up to George and said in this very bossy voice that they needed to talk."

"Hmm," said Sam.

"The thing was, she bumped into him in the process of sidling up. I thought at the time that maybe she didn't have great balance, in fact, I reached out to steady her. But what if she'd been using that as a way to put the almonds in George's food?"

"Pretty bold, doing that in front of you," said Sam.

"Yes. But that means it could be the perfect cover. None of us thought anything about it except that George and Nora didn't seem to like each other much. Do you think I should tell the police about it?"

Sam pursed her lips. "Why not? It'll give them another lead to work on. While you're doing that, I'm going to start reading through the old HOA emails from the last couple of years."

Chad winced. "That doesn't sound like a fun way to spend your afternoon."

"Well, it'll get the task off my list, and that part is pretty fun for me."

Chad said, "Shouldn't we celebrate? Maybe go out and get drinks? Find a place that's open on a Sunday? After all, you're Madam President now."

"Let's see how I do with the emails. Also, I want to send one of my own, regarding the movie night."

"Right. When is that again?" asked Chad.

"I'd originally thought about doing it next weekend, but everyone is always busy on the weekends. Soccer practice, grocery shopping, time with friends. It would be too easy for everyone to say they have something else to do. If no one shows up for my first Maple Hills event, it would set a bad precedent."

Chad considered this. "True. But aren't people also busy during the week? And tired?"

"Yes, but they still have time to watch TV, right? I thought I'd set it up so that it's fairly early . . . maybe 6:30 to 8:30. With any luck, they'll think of it as a nice break."

"So you're looking at doing this when?"

Sam smiled, but her eyes were tired. "There's no time like the present. I'm thinking tomorrow evening. Maybe it'll be a nice way for everybody to relax on a Monday."

Sam ended up being too busy to go out for those drinks. The old emails proved very interesting. George Turner's almond allergy was mentioned numerous times whenever there was any sort of picnic or potluck. There were pictures of previous Maple Hills events in the emailed newsletters, too. Sam spent quite some time poring over them. They often showed George and Nora on the opposite ends of the photo.

Sam looked carefully at one that showed George and Olivia in the same picture. They weren't standing together, but George was staring directly at Olivia, who was looking at the camera.

There was even a picture with the elusive Pris in it. She appeared to want to escape as soon as possible and was on the edge of the group. There was a stressed smile on her face. Interestingly, she was standing right beside Julia. In fact, Julia had thrown an arm around her. Perhaps that's why Pris looked as if she wanted to run away. Sam took time to update her murder scorecard before neatly filing it away in an accordion file.

Then she sat still for a few moments, feeling suddenly exhausted. She thought about Pris being blackmailed and Nora bumping into George at the picnic. She thought about the old newsletters she'd looked through. As she sat, her mood grew darker. When Arlo worriedly nuzzled his nose against her leg, she reached down to pick him up for a snuggle.

Another nice distraction from her dark mood came when she started getting emails regarding movie night. Her emailed invitation had gotten a lot more attention than she'd thought it might, considering the short notice. The nice thing, of course, about short notice was that if the event had been a flop, it wouldn't look so bad. From what she could tell, though, there was quite a bit of interest in coming. Some residents were planning on bringing food. It was going to be held at the neighborhood's clubhouse, which would make everything easier.

The next morning, Sam was trying to decide between streaming *E.T.* or *The Princess Bride* when the doorbell rang. Arlo leaped up off his bed, tail wagging excitedly. When she pulled open the door, Olivia Stanton was standing there, giving her a shy smile.

"Hi there!" said Sam. "Come on inside."

"I'm really sorry to intrude on you like this," said Olivia, hesitantly following Sam inside.

"Thanks again for the delicious food you made for us. Chad and I enjoyed it so much."

Olivia looked pleased. "Thanks for saying so. It's one of the things on my rotation at home." She glanced around and said in a low voice, "Is your husband around? I was hoping to have a word with you in private."

Sam said, "Let me find out exactly where he is, then we'll head off to a quiet nook." She listened at the door leading down to the basement and nodded. "He's in his man cave down there. Just the same, we'll find a spot to chat."

There was a sitting area that Sam hadn't even spent any time in yet. It was tucked away from the rest of the house and boasted plush, earth-toned upholstery, a large picture window looking out onto the rose garden outside, and walls lined with books. There was even a fireplace in there for cooler days.

"Wow, this is such a beautiful room," said Olivia.

Sam smiled at her. "Thanks. I'd take the credit, but we had a designer to come over before we moved in and she set everything up. I think the designer had originally envisioned this to be a hangout for Chad, but he seems to prefer spending all his time in the basement. Can I get you a glass of water? Or juice?"

Olivia quickly shook her head. "No, thank you. I really just needed someone to talk to. You'd think after living in Maple

Hills for five years that I'd have made more friends than I have. But I didn't seem to connect with anybody. The people I *have* connected with are too busy to spare much time."

"That sounds kind of lonely," said Sam.

"It has been sometimes," admitted Olivia. "That might be why I ended up in an affair with George to begin with. My husband goes off to work, I don't have a lot of connections here in town, and I was spending way too much time by myself." She shook her head. "Dom thinks I need to get out more. Invite some folks for coffee. But everybody else is so busy."

Sam nodded slowly. She was busy herself. But she didn't like to think that she wouldn't make the time to go have coffee with a friend.

Olivia flushed. "Anyway, sorry for bending your ear about that. The whole reason I came by is because you're the only person who knows about my affair with George. I can't talk about this with anybody else." She gave Sam an apologetic look.

Sam thought guiltily about Pris's neighbor, who'd definitely known about the affair. And Nora. But it really wouldn't help Olivia out to know that more people were aware of her relationship with George. It would likely just add to her stress. She said stoutly, "Of *course* you needed to come by and talk with me about it. I'm glad you did."

Olivia relaxed a little in her chair. "Thank you. I'm probably being paranoid, but I think the police are getting more and more suspicious of me. I'm sure they're planning on arresting me or exposing the affair. They've been relentless about dropping by and asking me questions. Dom is wondering why the cops keep wanting to speak with me. I've been having trouble eating and sleeping, too. I'm a mess." She gave a short laugh that threatened to turn into a sob.

"Are the police being careful about questioning you? I mean, are they talking to you in front of your husband?"

Olivia shook her head. "No, they've tried to be careful with that. A couple of times when they've been over, they've asked to speak with me alone. But you can see why that's making Dom even more suspicious. Then, after poor Julia died, they spoke to both of us at the same time, but didn't mention anything about George's and my affair."

"How did that work out?"

Olivia gave a helpless shrug. "Dom got so angry. He doesn't understand why the police keep talking to us. He's spoken to other neighbors and knows that the cops aren't questioning them like this. So he was getting belligerent. Then there was a problem with our alibis. They wanted to know where we were the night before Julia was found."

Sam nodded.

Olivia said, "I said I was at home with Dom that night and the morning of Julia's death. But Dom and I have totally different sleep schedules. Dom sleeps like the dead, so he told the cops he'd never know if I left."

Sam's eyes opened wide. "He said that?"

"He did. I think he's trying to get back at me, although he doesn't even know what for. And he gave me this suspicious look when he said it. He was wondering what the police were getting at." She paused, looking down at her hands. "And I wasn't entirely truthful before, mostly because I hate even thinking about it, much less talking about it. But George was actually trying to blackmail me about our affair."

This wasn't as much of a surprise as Olivia might have thought. Sam had already heard a similar story from Pris. Again, it seemed as if George enjoyed the power and control of forcing someone to pay up. He certainly didn't seem to have needed the money. "I'm so sorry," she said.

Olivia teared up a little, and Sam pulled a box of tissues closer. "*I'm* sorry. It's such a mess. I couldn't believe it when George threatened to expose our affair unless I started paying him. But he had nothing to lose. I was the one who could lose my husband. The thing is, he gave me the feeling it wasn't the first time he'd tried blackmailing somebody. It made me wonder if George used information for leverage to get his way on all sorts of things. Maybe HOA votes, networking, whatever. When we were having our affair, he'd make these kinds of veiled references to knowing all kinds of secrets about people in Maple Hills. It sounded like he might use them to his advantage."

"George sounds like he was a real piece of work."

Olivia gave another mirthless laugh. "I know. Believe me, he wasn't like that when we were in a relationship. I mean, I got hints of it. But mostly, he seemed like a great guy."

Sam remembered how Chad had said what a great guy George had seemed after he'd met him at the picnic. It sounded like George could make people believe he was a totally different person than the one he was. She also thought that Olivia seemed to be drawn to problematic men.

"Do you have any thoughts about what happened to Julia? And to George, of course."

Olivia sat quietly for a moment. "Well, I know I thought Marcus Turner might have been involved. But now, I'm seriously thinking about blackmail being the motive. That seems to take Marcus off the hook. I was wondering about Nora." She glanced up at Sam. "I know that sounds crazy, but she couldn't stand George. She lived right next door to him, too, and maybe George was able to get dirt on her somehow."

"Did the police indicate who they might be focusing on?"

Olivia said bitterly, "Besides me, you mean? No. I have no idea what they're thinking. But it's making me a nervous wreck. I have so many different emotions going through me all the time. My blood pressure is probably through the roof."

"I've read that it's helpful to talk about and label your feelings," said Sam slowly.

"Really? I'd like to think something would help, but it's hard to imagine."

Sam said, "It's supposed to help you look at your emotions through a filter. Give yourself some distance from them."

Olivia looked doubtful but said, "Okay, I'll give it a go. First off, I'm scared. I'm afraid Dom is going to find out I was cheating on him. Then he'll divorce me, and I'll be left trying to figure out my life. Starting over. Getting a job when I'm really not qualified to do anything."

"I can see where that would be scary."

Olivia thought about it some more. "Then I feel completely betrayed. I foolishly placed my trust in George, and he not only violated my trust, he blackmailed me. On top of that, his death has put me into potential legal trouble."

"Betrayal would be a big one, for sure. I'd imagine it would be hard to trust people again."

"Exactly," said Olivia. "It also makes me feel naïve for believing in George in the first place. Naïve or stupid."

"You were just lonely, like you said."

Olivia took a deep breath. "I'm also feeling incredibly anxious. My stomach is tied up in knots, my appetite is off, my drinking is up. I'm not exercising. Basically, I'm not doing any of the things that I know, intellectually, would help me feel better. At the same time, I'm frustrated with myself for having gotten into this position to begin with. I like to think of myself as smarter than this. But here I am, a suspect in a murder investigation after involving myself with a man who didn't have my best interests at heart."

Sam said, "I know the police are working hard to bring the killer to justice. Just try to remember that they can't arrest anyone without evidence."

Olivia's tight expression relaxed a little, and she gave Sam a small smile. "Thank you. You know, I actually feel a little better."

"You sound surprised," said Sam with a laugh.

"Well, experts always say it's good to talk about your problems, but I never really believed it. Just having this stuff bottled up inside me hasn't been good for me, though." She reached out and gave Sam a quick hug. "I appreciate it. And hey, sorry I haven't reached out about us finding volunteer opportunities to work on together. My head hasn't been in the right place."

"It's on my list of things to look at next week," said Sam with a grin. "Oh, and did you get the email about movie night tonight?"

Now Olivia looked as if she might want to escape. "I think I saw something in my inbox, yes. Sorry, I haven't gotten around to RSVPing."

"No need for that," said Sam briskly. "It's just an event for whoever can make it. It might help take your mind off things for a couple of hours. And who knows, you could end up making new friends there, too."

Olivia gave her a wry smile. "You're absolutely right, Sam. I'll try to make it tonight. Thanks so much."

Arlo helped Sam escort Olivia to the door. She reached down and loved on the little dog for a minute. "He's the sweetest thing. I'm so glad he's with you now."

Sam set out the door with packets of microwave popcorn. "See you later, Chad," she called at the door.

"How long do you think it'll run?" he asked.

"I'm guessing between set-up, take-down, any chatting, and the movie, I should be gone for three hours, give or take."

Chad said, "Sure you're okay with me not going? I can help, if you want?"

"No, that's fine. I'd rather use you for something more complicated," said Sam. She gave him a distracted smile.

"Gee, thanks," said Chad with a laugh.

The clubhouse was a nice hub for Maple Hills activities. It was an ample building with a classic brick and wood siding design. There was a spacious porch with rocking chairs and hanging flower baskets. The inside had comfortable furnishings and a versatile space for different neighborhood events. There was a kitchenette off to the side. Sam headed toward the big screen and started setting up for the movie. Once that was done, she made a few bowls of microwave popcorn to set out in the main room.

Sam was doing everything on autopilot, her mind whirring with all the different things she was thinking. She glanced at her watch. Hopefully, people would start showing up soon. That would help keep her mind on the topic at hand.

Fortunately, ten minutes later, neighbors started coming in. Mandy and Albert were the first ones there. Mandy gave her a hug and Albert did the same. "We're so excited that you're the new president!" Mandy said.

"Thanks! I'm excited, too. Hopefully, we can do more of these low-key events from time to time. How are things going for you? Any more trouble from the billing department?"

Albert shook his head, grinning broadly. "Nope. You fixed that problem for us. I gotta thank you again. I can't tell you how much time and energy we were pouring into that issue."

"It was my pleasure to take care of it," said Sam warmly. "Like I said, non-responsive customer service is one of my pet peeves."

Mandy said, "How is life treating *you*, Sam? Seems like things are going your way with the election and all."

"And Arlo," said Albert. "Guess you've got a very grateful little guy living with you."

And suddenly, to her horror, Sam thought she might cry. Crying was something that was definitely *never* on her list of things to do. Maybe that's why it tried to sneak out of her at the worst possible times.

Mandy and Albert were frowning worriedly at her.

"Something's wrong," said Mandy, reaching out to Sam.

"Just let me know and I'll take care of it for you," said Albert with a dark look that boded ill for anybody causing Sam trouble.

Sam quickly rubbed her eyes, hoping to keep the moisture in them from spilling out. "So silly of me," she said with a laugh. "You know, I think it's just been so busy lately. Maybe I haven't been getting the sleep I need."

"Sleep is so important," agreed Mandy, rubbing Sam's arms. "Please take care of yourself."

Albert looked a bit more doubtful that Sam's tears could be attributed to a lack of sleep. "If you find out that sleep isn't the problem, let me know."

Sam gave them both a smile. "You're the best." She glanced around at the nearly full room with a look of satisfaction. "Well, I guess I better get the ball rolling so we can stay on time."

She'd decided on *The Princess Bride* in the end, thinking it might be a crowd-pleaser. She got everyone's attention. "Thanks so much for coming out this evening for movie night. I'm hoping to do more of these laid-back events to give us a chance to know our neighbors better."

Then Sam blanked out and had no idea what she'd planned on saying. She fumbled to find her notecards, dropping a few of them on the floor in the process. Albert leaped up and retrieved them for her, giving her that anxious look again. She smiled at him, cleared her throat, and continued. "Tonight, we're going to watch an old favorite, *The Princess Bride*. I'm sure it needs no introduction." She went on, with the help of her notecards, to thank everyone for supporting her in the recent election. Then she jotted down her phone number on a nearby white board and reminded her neighbors to let her know if they needed anything.

"There's popcorn in the kitchenette, along with some water bottles. Please feel free to help yourself."

Everyone clapped and Sam started the film. Then she settled herself in the back of the room, waiting until the movie was about ten minutes in. Then she slipped out, typing on her phone as she did.

The sun was going down, but there was still plenty of light to see by. She headed home quickly, her body tense as she went. She knew what she'd see. But, at the same time, she didn't want to see it. She hoped she was wrong.

She strode up her long driveway to her house at the top of the hill. She crept over to the side to look into the living room window. There, sure enough, was exactly what she expected to see. Chad and Pris, embracing on the living room sofa.

Chapter Sixteen

She closed her eyes briefly, then squared her shoulders and headed for the door. She paused, briefly, to pull out the hammer she'd hidden earlier from the potted plants, sticking it in her purse, which she'd brought along with her. Then she walked inside.

Chad and Pris jerked back away from each other, shock on their faces.

"You're here," spluttered Chad. "What are you doing here? Aren't you helping with movie night?"

Pris stared at her stonily, not saying a word.

"Yes, I *was* helping out there. I stepped away a few minutes to come home and find what I thought I'd find . . . the two of you together. You look very cozy on the sofa," said Sam, her mouth twisting.

"Look, I can explain," said Chad. "This isn't what it looks like."

"Isn't it?" asked Sam sweetly. "I've always heard that looks can be deceiving, but this is one instance where they really aren't. Let me set this up for you, how I see it. Then you can tell me if it's still not what it looks like."

Chad was silent, and Pris stared at her with those emotionless eyes.

Sam took a deep breath, edging closer to the two. "First off, I think you two had a pretty ingenious plan. I'm guessing the end goal was to get rid of me, although I'm not totally sure how you were planning on doing it."

Chad gave a strangled laugh. "Why would you think that? Sam, you're confused here. You're acting paranoid."

"No, I'm actually seeing everything clearly for the first time in a while. It's funny how you can look at something in a particular way. But then, when you look at it from a different angle, everything changes."

Chad tilted his head to one side. "Sweetheart, I don't know what you're talking about. Have you been drinking?"

"No, I've never been more clearheaded in my life. I remember when I was talking with Julia, shortly before her death. I felt like she seemed really tense through our conversation. Naturally, I'd chalked it up to George's death at the picnic and the police questioning her. But looking back, she was asking a good number of questions about us, Chad."

Chad gave her a pleading look. "Sam, what do you mean? Of course she was. That's the polite thing to do when you're talking to someone who just moved into the neighborhood." He stood up, arms outstretched as if to draw her in, but Sam stepped backward.

"Yes, of course, that's polite. But her manner was sharper. It wasn't small talk. She was especially curious to know if we moved to the area from somewhere else or whether we were new to Maple Hills instead of to the area."

"Okay, right. But that makes sense, too, Sam. Those are exactly the kinds of questions you ask someone who's just moved in."

Sam continued. "The reason Julia was so curious is because she couldn't figure out why you, a complete stranger to George Turner, would have murdered him. She *saw* you, Chad. But what she saw didn't make any sense to her. Julia probably even heard George introduce himself, so she knew you weren't acquainted with him. You shouldn't have had a reason in the world to kill him. But she knew. And that's why you killed her."

"This is preposterous! Samantha, are you listening to yourself?"

Sam looked over at Pris, who seemed wary but composed. "Pris, of course, *did* have a motive to kill George. But she had the perfect alibi for the picnic, despite the attention the police were giving her. She was clearly on the fringes of the picnic, too nervous to join in. Multiple people noticed that. You were nowhere near George's quinoa salad, Pris. Which is why the two of you made such a good team. Chad with no motive and Pris with no access to the victim."

Sam saw a bit of movement out of the corner of her eye. She didn't dare lose focus on Chad and Pris, though. She took a deep breath to steady her nerves.

Pris gave Sam a look of dislike. "And so you think Chad killed George for me?"

"No, I think Chad killed George for *himself*. I think Chad killed George because George was going to spill the beans that you and Chad were having an affair. George didn't know Chad—he'd never met him. But he already knew about your

DWI and was threatening to disclose that. George probably thought that telling everyone you were having some sort of illicit affair would be icing on the cake. But as soon as he mentioned it to you, Pris, he sealed his fate."

"This is all very dramatic," said Chad with a short laugh, taking another step toward Sam. She took another one away from him.

"Nora had an interesting perspective. When the police were questioning her after Julia's death, she said the reason she'd been trying to get in touch with Julia is because she suspected Julia had murdered George. She said it was because she was staring at George a lot during the picnic." Sam paused. "But what I think Julia was staring at was Chad slipping almonds into George's food."

"Why didn't she go to the police, then?" asked Pris in that strikingly cold, calm way.

"I'm guessing that she was trying to give Chad the benefit of the doubt. She'd already heard from me that Chad and I had no connection to Maple Hills or Sunset Ridge. She couldn't figure out why Chad would have done such a thing. Maybe she thought her eyes were playing tricks on her. She was a careful sort of person, someone who was a planner. She would have wanted to speak with Chad before making accusations to the police."

Now it was Chad's turn to sound cold. "You know, this is really insulting. You're making all sorts of allegations. I'm your husband. We've been together for a long time. I told you there's a reasonable explanation for all this."

"One reasonable explanation is that the two of you were having an affair. You decided you could get rid of me, marry, and live comfortably." The words stung as Sam forced them out of her mouth.

Chad said, "Kill you? Is that what you're saying? As if there was no other option? What about divorce, if I'm so tired of you?"

"Because you couldn't continue living the lifestyle you've become accustomed to," said Sam, sounding as tired as she felt. She glanced over at Pris. "There were some inconsistencies with you, you know."

Pris quirked an eyebrow.

"You said you'd never met Julia. But I found a picture of the two of you, arms around each other, in the newsletter archive for Maple Hills."

Pris shrugged. "My memory has never been that great."

"Also, you allegedly hadn't met my husband, although clearly you have."

Pris nodded at her as if conceding that point.

"When I borrowed your phone the other day, Chad, I saw some interesting information on it," said Sam, looking steadily at her husband.

"Hey, I don't know what you're talking about. There's nothing on that phone."

"Oh, I'm sure you're doing your texting to each other on a burner phone. No, I'm talking about your Google location data. It indicated that you spent quite a bit of time at Pris's house prior to us moving to Maple Hills."

Chad flushed. "But that's absurd. I didn't even know Pris."

"Is it? Google begs to differ. And I could also point out that you got a new car before we moved here. I'm guessing that's because your old car was recognizable to neighbors."

Chad was quiet. "Checking out my location data means you didn't trust me."

"I did. Until I had good reason not to. Did you forget I was in the tech industry?" She gave him a sad look. "You didn't even try very hard to cover it up."

"You're so busy," said Pris with another shrug. "Chad probably thought you wouldn't notice."

Sam said, "I could match up the times Chad was at your house last summer with times on my calendar when I was out volunteering for the day. So yes, I guess being busy factored into enabling your affair." She turned to Chad again. "You recently suddenly 'remembered' that Nora had bumped into George at the picnic, allegedly causing a distraction to give herself the opportunity to tamper with George's salad."

"So?"

"So, for you to have witnessed that, it obviously had to be when you and I were at the picnic. I had eyes on Nora the whole time. She never approached George while we were there."

Chad rolled his eyes. "Maybe someone told me about the incident."

"Or maybe you were trying to divert attention from yourself."

"It's still not much evidence," said Chad sulkily.

"Also, Arlo hates you both," said Sam. "Where is he, by the way?"

"We stuck him upstairs and closed the door." Chad's demeanor changed. "Okay, I'm done with this. It's over, Sam. It wasn't supposed to go this way, but that can't be helped." He moved closer again, and again, Sam stepped further back. Chad said to Pris, "Go upstairs to the bedroom and grab Sam's jewelry. It's in a case in the closet."

"Dumb," said Sam. "Hopefully, the original plan was brighter than this one, or you were doomed to fail. You're thinking of staging a robbery gone wrong, aren't you?"

Chad looked at her through narrowed eyes.

"The police will dust for fingerprints. Pris's fingerprints will be everywhere. Also, when I don't show back up at the end of the movie, people will wonder where I am. They'll come looking for me. And where exactly are *you* supposed to be? You weren't at movie night."

Chad appeared to be thinking quickly. "I'll say I was out running errands, then joined movie night late. I'll be confused about where you are. I'll say you weren't at home."

"But I *am* at home," pointed out Sam.

"I'll say I didn't *see* you. Your body will have to be somewhere out of sight."

"You'll never get away with this, Chad. There are too many issues. Remember, it takes a Type-A person to carry out murder successfully. You're Type-B, at best."

Chad leaned down and unplugged the phone chargers from an extension cord. Then he held the long extension cord in front of him as Pris started for the staircase to plunder Sam's jewelry box.

"This might be a good time to mention that I hit 911 before walking into the house," said Sam calmly. "Because I *am* Type-A." She'd also hit the record button on her voice recorder, a fact she didn't mention.

"Nice bluff," said Chad.

Sam was about to pull the hammer from her purse when the front door burst open. Alfred was standing there, burly and infuriated. "Drop it," he said to Chad.

Chad gaped at him. "Who are you?"

"Drop it!"

But Chad, never one to follow directions very well, didn't. Instead, he grabbed his car keys from the coffee table and bolted for the front door. He stopped with a jerk when he encountered Mandy, who appeared to be videoing him with her phone. He snarled at her, raising his hand to dash the device to the floor.

Alfred bellowed, charging at Chad and tackling him. He whaled at him with his fists a few times, for good measure.

Then, the reassuring sound of sirens signaled the imminent arrival of the police.

Chad slumped to the floor, defeated.

Chapter Seventeen

Mandy's phone wasn't broken, which was very helpful, considering all the video she'd recorded from outside the house. Sam's audio was nice and clear, as well. Pris had tried to slip away through the back door, but was quickly intercepted by a cheerful cop. Mandy rescued Arlo from an upstairs bedroom, crooning to the little dog as she gently placed him in Sam's lap for a snuggle.

Mandy was fussing over Sam, throwing a blanket around her shoulders and bringing her a cup of chamomile tea. "You poor thing," she clucked.

Alfred was pacing around, still very keyed up. He appeared to be ready to engage in any altercation that might be thrown at him, although life seemed much more under control, with Chad and Pris now sitting in the backs of separate police vehicles.

Sam made a quick phone call to Olivia.

"Sam?" she asked. "Everything okay?"

Sam carefully considered that question. Her husband had planned on murdering her. She'd been betrayed in the worst possible way. But still, she felt somehow that it was all going to be okay in the end. It was something she could get past. "Actually, yes. Yes, I think everything is fine. The only problem is that I had to leave movie night and now I can't return. This is a huge favor to ask, but could you possibly wrap things up over there for me? Thank everyone for coming and apologize for my absence? I had to get back home and got detained."

Olivia said, "Of course I will. You're sure everything is all right?"

"Yes, I think so. The good news is that you're not a suspect anymore."

"Really?" Olivia's voice lightened. "The police made an arrest?"

"Two of them, actually. I'll have to tell you about it tomorrow," she said as the detective, Warren Watson, walked into the room. "I should go." Sam hung up, glad she'd wrapped up movie night and gotten Olivia to socialize all at the same time.

Watson looked tired, but alert. He spoke briefly to the other police officers before coming over to the sitting area. Sam perched on the very edge of the sofa with her hot tea. Mandy was still fussing over her nearby. Alfred finally stopped pacing and settled down in an armchair when Watson joined them. But he looked as if he might leap from the chair at any time and start subduing more unruly characters.

"Now," said Watson. "I know this has been a rough evening for all of you. Especially you, Ms. Prescott."

Sam was suddenly very glad that she hadn't taken Chad's last name when they married. "An unsettling evening, yes." Arlo leaned back against her chest, and she slowly rubbed him.

"But not, maybe, entirely a shock," said Watson slowly.

"Maybe not," admitted Sam.

"All right. We'll circle back around to that shortly. I'd like to hear from the two of you, please, before we do." Watson looked down at his notes before giving up trying to find their names in his notebook. "Could you remind me of your names?"

Mandy and Alfred did.

"And what made you decide to come over to the Prescott house?"

Mandy started. "Well, we were all over at movie night in the Maple Hills clubhouse. Sam is our new HOA president, and she'd set it all up. It was *The Princess Bride*, a lovely movie."

Alfred smiled at her. "We'll have to rent it this weekend to watch."

Mandy smiled back at him. "Anyway, Sam had everything set up, and the neighbors were there. But she didn't seem like herself. She's usually so sharp, so on top of things. But she seemed really distracted. And a bit teary."

Alfred chipped in, "She lost her place when she was giving a little speech to welcome everyone there." He turned to Sam. "Sorry to mention it. You set up a nice movie night. But you weren't acting like yourself."

"No, I'm delighted you noticed," said Sam. She gave a small shiver, thinking of herself up against Chad with her hammer.

Mandy said, "I thought she might not be feeling well. She was pale, you know. Then we saw her slip out after the movie started. We decided to follow her."

Watson tilted his head to one side. "That seems a little extreme."

Alfred shook his head. "You don't understand. Sam had helped us out with a very sticky problem we'd been dealing with.

We wanted to return the favor. We knew something was wrong, whether she was sick, or whether there was something else going on. So we followed her."

"We could tell she was going home. We just didn't know why. She'd been all excited about winning the HOA spot and having a movie night. Why would she leave? Then we saw her, outside her house, peering in through the window." Mandy gestured to the offending window.

Alfred stepped in. "So, as soon as Sam went inside, we did the same thing."

"I taped everything on my phone," said Mandy. "Although my hands were shaking so bad that I'm not sure how great the video is."

Watson looked over at Sam. "I believe Ms. Prescott made an audiotape of what transpired inside."

"The two tapes should be all you need," said Alfred. "I couldn't believe what I was seeing." He curled up his fists as his face reddened, remembering.

Mandy said, "Alfred wanted to go in there right away, as soon as we saw Pris and Chad together. He was going to toss both of them out and then change the locks on Sam's door for her."

"I've got some old locks that would do fine," said Alfred darkly. His face seemed to indicate that some of his old locks might have gone to trapping Chad in a dark basement somewhere.

"But I stopped him," said Mandy. She looked at Sam. "I thought that's what you might want . . . to collect as much evidence as possible. Because, when I saw Pris and Chad together, I realized they might have ganged up to murder George and Julia. Although I don't have any idea why."

"We'll get to that in a minute, too," said Watson. "What I'd like to know is what you saw that made you decide to go inside."

Alfred took a deep breath. "Well, we saw Chad walking toward Sam. He had unplugged some stuff from an extension cord and was about to wrap it around her neck." His beefy hands were in fists again. "That's all it took."

Arlo leaned back and licked Sam on the chin.

"I kept videoing," said Mandy helpfully. "You can see it on the tape."

"And Pris Lawrence?" asked Watson. "What was she doing while this was going on?"

Alfred waved his hand. "Oh, he'd sent her off upstairs for some reason."

Sam cleared her throat. "He was planning to make my death look like a burglary gone wrong. He'd sent Pris upstairs to take my jewelry."

Alfred glowered at this.

Sam said, "I told him it was a poor way to set up a murder. That he'd never get away with it. Sure enough, he didn't."

Watson jotted down a few more notes. "All right. Now I think I'd like to hear about how this whole evening came to be. Sam, it sounds like you already realized your husband was having an affair."

Sam looked down at her hands, which were shaking just the smallest bit. Mandy reached over and patted them, looking concerned. Sam smiled at her, then said, "I did. But I needed more than my own suspicions. I mean, I *knew*, but I wanted more proof."

Watson said, "So was the movie night a set-up so you could catch your husband and Pris Lawrence together?"

"Very intuitive of you. It was, yes, partially. But it was also there so that I could start out my HOA role with a fun event. If you're asking if I told Chad how long I'd be gone, the answer is yes. I had the feeling that he'd have Pris over here as soon as I left the house."

Watson jotted that down. "How did you find out about the affair?"

"Gradually. It wasn't something Chad had ever done before, to my knowledge. But after our move, I felt like Chad was just out of the house a lot."

"That wasn't usual for him?"

"No," said Sam. "Chad's always been a big homebody. His idea of a good day is spending time in the basement playing video games. So this was a departure from the norm, for sure."

"A change of behavior. Right. But you must have had more than that to go off of."

"Sure," said Sam. "I thought the change of vehicle before we moved to Maple Hills was interesting. Chad loved that Range Rover, and it would have been a great car for the mountains. But I started wondering if he'd been seeing someone in the neighborhood. Perhaps neighbors would have noticed his Range Rover going to Pris's house. It made sense that he'd be eager to change it out for something else before we moved here. But that's not all I was going off of."

Watson gave her a quizzical look.

"I went into Chad's phone to check his location timeline. Chad's never been a big tech person, so I knew he'd never think to take location tracking off."

Mandy said, "But wouldn't he try to keep you from seeing his phone? Wouldn't he have text messages and stuff from Pris on there?" She put her hand over her mouth as Watson looked irked.

"Chad wasn't *that* clueless. He had a burner phone for communicating with Pris. At least, I'm assuming he did."

Watson nodded. "We found it on him."

"So he didn't think twice about handing his main phone over to me. He told me his phone was acting very sluggish and asked if I could help speed up the performance. He also was running out of storage space on the device."

Watson said slowly, "Chad knew you were good at technology?"

"Yes. That's the line of work I'd been in before."

Watson looked thoughtfully at Sam. "I see. I was wondering about your will. If that's something you'd made or not. I know you're young, but I thought you might have already had one made."

Alfred snorted. "You're asking *Sam* this? She's the most organized person I know. She probably had a will when she was a teenager."

Sam smiled at Alfred. "I was in my early-twenties when I had it made. When I was engaged to Chad."

Watson said, "I'm assuming you intended on leaving a substantial amount to your husband."

"Aside from what I was giving to charity, yes. All of it. I don't have a relationship with my family, and Chad and I didn't have children. Most of it was going to him."

Mandy shook her head, looking angry. "That man."

Watson said, "And you've been married for a while. It's not as if you've been together for a couple of years."

"We've been married for a decade," said Sam, looking sad. "That's probably what hurts the most. We've had what I thought was a good marriage. Now I'm looking at it from a totally different perspective. I'm thinking that everything I thought was real was actually a lie all along. That I was fooling myself."

Watson shook his head, looking a little uncomfortable in the role of comforter. "No. Don't think that way. He seems to have been a very capable actor. When did you realize that things were off? When did you suspect Chad?"

"Gradually. Too gradually. Maybe I was blind out of a sense of self-preservation. After Julia died, I mulled over what we'd talked about before her death. It seemed like a pretty normal conversation, but the more I thought about it, the more things seemed to stand out. She was interested in whether we'd lived in the Sunset Ridge area for long. That might sound like she was trying to make conversation, as I thought it was at the time. But looking back, she was very intent. Laser-focused. As if she were trying to figure out why Chad would have put nuts in George's salad."

"I don't get why she didn't go to the cops right away," said Mandy.

"I have the feeling she wanted to be sure. She didn't want to just throw Chad under the bus. Maybe she thought her eyes were playing tricks on her. I'm guessing she contacted Chad to see if there was anything there." Sam shook her head angrily. "She should have thrown him under the bus, as she'd planned to before. She'd still be alive today."

Sam looked at Watson. "I have a question for you, actually. I know you have audio and video footage of what happened. But when the case goes to a jury, it's usually good if there's physical evidence, too. Do you have anything like that? Something to make the case against Pris and Chad airtight?"

Watson said, "Well, I can't disclose too much, under the circumstances. But we have hopes we might make a match for some hair and fibers we found at the scene at Julia Harper's house. We're going to remove some of your husband's belongings shortly for examination by the lab. His laptop too, of course, which we hope might have some other evidence on it."

Sam gave a satisfied bob of her head. "Good. It sounds like you'll have enough."

Alfred said, "I don't know a lot about this, but will Pris be charged the same way? It's sounding like she might not have killed either George or Julia."

"She's being charged as an accessory at this point. But of course, we may learn more as the investigation progresses."

Sam said, "Is it all right if I stay here tonight? At the house, I mean? Will I be in the way?"

Watson said, "Fortunately, this is *not* a crime scene. After we remove your husband's belongings, we'll get out of here."

"Are you sure you want to stay here, Sam?" asked Mandy, looking anxious. "You could stay at our place."

Alfred jumped in. "We have a guest room that's ready to go. You just say the word."

Sam smiled at them. Despite the early hour, she felt as if she was shutting down. She would barely be able to keep her eyes open soon. "Thanks, both of you. But I think what I'm going to do is reclaim this space." She looked down at Arlo, who was sleeping in her lap with his head on her arm. "With Arlo."

Mandy stood up. "Gotcha. Well, let Alfred and me know if you need anything at all. We're going to get out of your way." She gave Sam a fierce hug, and she and Alfred headed home.

1. *Set up a neighborhood meeting to talk about what happened. Give reassurances.*
2. *Take a trip with Arlo. The beach? It's still warm for September.*
3. *Have an estate sale to get rid of Chad's remaining belongings.*
4. *Get a divorce lawyer.*

About the Author

Elizabeth writes the Southern Quilting mysteries and Memphis Barbeque mysteries for Penguin Random House and the Myrtle Clover series for Midnight Ink and independently. She blogs at ElizabethSpannCraig.com/blog, named by Writer's Digest as one of the 101 Best Websites for Writers. Elizabeth makes her home in Matthews, North Carolina, with her husband. She's the mother of two.

Sign up for Elizabeth's free newsletter to stay updated on releases:

https://bit.ly/2xZUXqO

This and That

Thanks for reading this first book in the Sunset Ridge series! If you'd like to stay informed on my releases, sign up for my free newsletter at https://bit.ly/2xZUXqO . You can unsubscribe at any time.

I love hearing from my readers. You can find me on Facebook as Elizabeth Spann Craig Author, on Twitter/X as elizabethscraig, on my website at elizabethspanncraig.com[1], and by email at elizabethspanncraig@gmail.com.

Thanks so much for reading my book...I appreciate it. If you enjoyed the story, would you please leave a short review on the site where you purchased it? Just a few words would be great. Not only do I feel encouraged reading them, but they also help other readers discover my books. Thank you!

Did you know my books are available in print and ebook formats? Most of the Myrtle Clover series is available in audio and some of the Southern Quilting mysteries are. Find the audiobooks here.[2]

1. http://elizabethspanncraig.com/
2. https://elizabethspanncraig.com/audio/

Please follow me on BookBub[3] for my reading recommendations and release notifications.

I'd also like to thank some folks who helped me put this book together. Thanks to my cover designer, Karri Klawiter, for her awesome covers. Thanks to my editor, Judy Beatty for her help. Thanks to beta readers Amanda Arrieta, Rebecca Wahr, Cassie Kelley and Dan Harris for all of their helpful suggestions and careful reading. Thanks to my ARC readers for helping to spread the word. Thanks, as always, to my family and readers.

3. https://www.bookbub.com/profile/elizabeth-spann-craig?follow=true

Other Works by Elizabeth

Myrtle Clover Series in Order (be sure to look for the Myrtle series in audio[1], ebook, and print[2]):

Pretty is as Pretty Dies[3]

Progressive Dinner Deadly[4]

A Dyeing Shame[5]

A Body in the Backyard[6]

Death at a Drop-In[7]

A Body at Book Club[8]

Death Pays a Visit[9]

A Body at Bunco[10]

---

1. **http://elizabethspanncraig.com/audiobooks/**
2. **https://docs.google.com/document/d/1bZOmP3h2hYct0WZ_mLMCRT-tjQWEIZuAwSFU82uvy1EE/edit?usp=sharing**
3. http://elizabethspanncraig.com/books/pretty-is-as-pretty-dies/
4. http://elizabethspanncraig.com/books/progressive-dinner-deadly/
5. http://elizabethspanncraig.com/books/a-dyeing-shame/
6. http://elizabethspanncraig.com/books/a-body-in-the-backyard/
7. http://elizabethspanncraig.com/books/death-at-a-drop-in/
8. http://elizabethspanncraig.com/books/a-body-at-book-club/
9. http://elizabethspanncraig.com/books/death-pays-a-visit/

Murder on Opening Night[11]
Cruising for Murder[12]
Cooking is Murder[13]
A Body in the Trunk[14]
Cleaning is Murder[15]
Edit to Death[16]
Hushed Up[17]
A Body in the Attic[18]
Murder on the Ballot[19]
Death of a Suitor[20]
A Dash of Murder[21]
Death at a Diner[22]
A Myrtle Clover Christmas[23]
Murder at a Yard Sale[24]

---

10. http://elizabethspanncraig.com/books/a-body-at-bunco/
11. http://elizabethspanncraig.com/books/murder-on-opening-night/
12. http://elizabethspanncraig.com/books/3920/
13. http://elizabethspanncraig.com/books/cooking-is-murder-a-myrtle-clover-cozy-mystery-coming-in-2017/
14. http://elizabethspanncraig.com/books/a-body-in-the-trunk/
15. http://elizabethspanncraig.com/books/cleaning-is-murder/
16. http://elizabethspanncraig.com/books/edit-to-death/
17. https://elizabethspanncraig.com/books/hushed-up/
18. https://elizabethspanncraig.com/a-body-in-the-attic/
19. https://elizabethspanncraig.com/murder-on-the-ballot/
20. https://elizabethspanncraig.com/death-of-a-suitor/
21. https://elizabethspanncraig.com/a-dash-of-murder/
22. https://elizabethspanncraig.com/death-at-a-diner/
23. https://elizabethspanncraig.com/a-myrtle-clover-christmas/

Doom and Bloom[25]
A Toast to Murder[26]

SOUTHERN QUILTING MYSTERIES in Order:

Quilt or Innocence[27]
Knot What it Seams[28]
Quilt Trip[29]
Shear Trouble[30]
Tying the Knot[31]
Patch of Trouble[32]
Fall to Pieces[33]
Rest in Pieces[34]
On Pins and Needles[35]
Fit to be Tied[36]

---

24. https://elizabethspanncraig.com/murder-at-yard-sale/
25. https://elizabethspanncraig.com/doom-and-bloom/
26. https://elizabethspanncraig.com/a-toast-to-murder/
27. http://elizabethspanncraig.com/books/quilt-or-innocence/
28. http://elizabethspanncraig.com/books/knot-what-it-seams/
29. http://elizabethspanncraig.com/books/quilt-trip/
30. http://elizabethspanncraig.com/books/shear-trouble/
31. http://elizabethspanncraig.com/books/tying-the-knot/
32. http://elizabethspanncraig.com/books/patch-of-trouble/
33. http://elizabethspanncraig.com/books/fall-to-pieces/
34. http://elizabethspanncraig.com/books/rest-in-pieces/
35. http://elizabethspanncraig.com/books/on-pins-and-needles/
36. https://elizabethspanncraig.com/books/fit-to-be-tied/

Embroidering the Truth[37]
Knot a Clue[38]
Quilt-Ridden[39]
Needled to Death[40]
A Notion to Murder[41]
Crosspatch[42]
Behind the Seams[43]
Quilt Complex[44]
A Southern Quilting Christmas (Oct. 2024)

The Village Library Mysteries in Order

Checked Out[45]
Overdue[46]
Borrowed Time[47]
Hush-Hush[48]
Where There's a Will[49]
Frictional Characters[50]

---

37. https://elizabethspanncraig.com/books/embroidering-the-truth/
38. https://elizabethspanncraig.com/knot-a-clue/
39. https://elizabethspanncraig.com/quilt-ridden/
40. https://elizabethspanncraig.com/?page_id=11372
41. https://elizabethspanncraig.com/a-notion-to-murder/
42. https://elizabethspanncraig.com/crosspatch/
43. https://elizabethspanncraig.com/behind-seams/
44. https://elizabethspanncraig.com/quilt-complex/
45. https://elizabethspanncraig.com/books/checked-out/
46. https://elizabethspanncraig.com/books/overdue/
47. https://elizabethspanncraig.com/borrowed-time/
48. https://elizabethspanncraig.com/hush-hush/
49. https://elizabethspanncraig.com/where-theres-a-will/

Spine Tingling[51]
A Novel Idea[52]
End of Story[53]
Booked Up[54]

MEMPHIS BARBEQUE MYSTERIES in Order (Written as Riley Adams):

Delicious and Suspicious[55]
Finger Lickin' Dead[56]
Hickory Smoked Homicide[57]
Rubbed Out[58]

And a standalone "cozy zombie" novel: Race to Refuge[59], written as Liz Craig

---

50. https://elizabethspanncraig.com/frictional-characters/
51. https://elizabethspanncraig.com/spine-tingling/
52. https://elizabethspanncraig.com/a-novel-idea/
53. https://elizabethspanncraig.com/end-of-story/
54. https://elizabethspanncraig.com/booked-up/
55. http://elizabethspanncraig.com/books/delicious-and-suspicious/
56. http://elizabethspanncraig.com/books/finger-lickin-dead/
57. http://elizabethspanncraig.com/memphis-barbeque-cozy-mysteries/hickory-smoked-homicide/
58. http://elizabethspanncraig.com/books/rubbed-out/
59. http://elizabethspanncraig.com/books/race-to-refuge/

Milton Keynes UK
Ingram Content Group UK Ltd.
UKHW022144010424
440421UK00014BA/734

9 781955 395328